Man, he had never had it this bad

Zach knew nothing about her. Marnie could be a thief trying to break in to the apartment. But he didn't care. Zach forced himself to turn back to taking off the door hinges. He had to get a grip. Moments later the door was off and Marnie ran into the room.

"I am so cold!" She raced over to the bed and pulled on the socks that lay rolled in a ball on the floor by a pair of ugly brown hiking boots.

It was the sexiest thing he'd ever seen.

Before he could stop himself, he'd knelt down and taken one of her feet, rubbing it between both hands.

"That tingles."

"Tingles are good." He smiled up at her and switched to a slow, deep kneading, concentrating on her toes and the ball of her foot. And maybe her leg and the sexy curve of her calf and how her skirt kept climbing northward…

Marnie let out a tiny, devastating moan. "That feels so good. You could do this for a living."

He could do this forever, Zach realized with a jolt.

Dear Reader,

The skirt is back, and guess who's got it? Franco! Yes, the doorman from the second installment of the SINGLE IN THE CITY books has broken up with his boyfriend and now owns a beautiful apartment in one of San Francisco's Victorian Painted Ladies. Franco plans to research the skirt's powers and write a script for a film or a play—he isn't particular. For inspiration (and money) he resumes his doorman profession and rents the apartment piecemeal to three new heroines who definitely need the skirt—only, Franco doesn't tell them that the skirt he lends them has the special power to attract their one true love. Can the skirt work if the wearer doesn't know about it?

I hope you enjoy the adventures of the latest SINGLE IN THE CITY heroines and follow along as Franco writes his script in the following books: *Engaging Alex* by Kristin Gabriel in June and *Flirting with Temptation* by Cara Summers in July. For more information about the SINGLE IN THE CITY series, please visit our Web site at www.singleinthecity.org. You can find me at www.HeatherMacAllister.com.

Warmly,

Heather MacAllister

The SINGLE IN THE CITY miniseries

860—MOONSTRUCK IN MANHATTAN—Cara Summers (December 2001)
864—TEMPTED IN TEXAS—Heather MacAllister (January 2002)
868—SEDUCED IN SEATTLE—Kristin Gabriel (February 2002)
892—SKIRTING THE ISSUE—Heather MacAllister (August 2002)
896—SHEERLY IRRESISTIBLE—Kristin Gabriel (September 2002)
900—SHORT, SWEET AND SEXY—Cara Summers (October 2002)
SINGLE IN SAN FRANCISCO—Cara Summers, an eHarlequin online read (August 2002)

Heather MacAllister

Male Call

TORONTO • NEW YORK • LONDON
AMSTERDAM • PARIS • SYDNEY • HAMBURG
STOCKHOLM • ATHENS • TOKYO • MILAN • MADRID
PRAGUE • WARSAW • BUDAPEST • AUCKLAND

To Peggy Field and Sue Pellegrino-Wolf
With Alpha Gam love

ISBN 0-373-69128-9

MALE CALL

This edition published by arrangement with Harlequin Books S.A.

Visit us at www.eHarlequin.com

Printed in U.S.A.

Prologue

MY DEAR MRS. HIGGENBOTHAM,
Greetings from sunny and windy San Francisco! I do hope you and Pierre are in the throes of connubial bliss. I want to hear all the details of the wedding, particularly in regard to the jewelry and gowns. I so wish I could have been there in New York, however it was time to move on. I do miss the city and the apartment building and your own dear self, though.

I cannot stress how much your friendship has meant to me during the trying times of late. Both Marlon and I thought we would be together forever and for my part, I did nothing to threaten that. I had invested all of myself. I'd spent my days looking after Marlon's building and tenants only to have him...but that is water under the bridge, as you know. It is sad when courts must become involved to protect those of us who have given all to a relationship. One would assume there would be an equitable distribution of assets with the understanding that there cannot be a monetary value placed on some contributions. Apparently my contributions were only worth one modest apartment in San Francisco.

Yet, I am not bitter. At least I now have a home. Marlon's apartment—former apartment, as I have recently received the deed—is one of four in a charming pink-and-green

Painted Lady, which is what we San Franciscans call the Victorian houses.

This one and its neighbors survived the great earthquake, though since construction began on the house across the street, I feel as though I relive the quake daily.

The apartment is furnished in period style—Marlon always did have exquisite taste—with a bedroom, office where I can work on my script and a largish kitchen. Oh, and a balcony, a cozy place where I can sit and watch the activity on Mission Street as I answer the call of my muse.

And speaking of that, I cannot express my gratitude to you for the gift of the skirt.

As my muse appears to have remained in New York, I shall continue with my study of the effects of the skirt on heterosexual mating. I find the subject fascinating, if perplexing, and I do believe there is a story here. Urban legends are always popular in movies and plays. The very idea that this nondescript, though well-tailored, black skirt has some sort of power to attract men is preposterous and yet A.J., Sam and Claire, and even your dear self all swear it's true. And have you heard from the girls? I do miss them. Is all well with them? Sam, especially, was a valuable source of gossip.

I have decided to put the skirt to the test. As it happens, I find myself short of cash. Not to worry! The residents of this building and the others on the block have never known the convenience of a doorman until now. For a small honorarium, I have offered my services to deal with repairmen and accept packages and keep an eye on the neighborhood. But until my talents as an actor and playwright are recognized, I must provide my own backing. Therefore, I have removed to the service quarters in the basement and am attempting to rent out the apartment on a daily basis to those who need a temporary base in the city.

No, do not feel sorry for me, Mrs. H. One must suffer for one's art, though I seem to suffer more than most. But my plan is to rent to single young ladies who can make use of the skirt—and who will recount all their adventures to me. Perhaps my muse will be intrigued enough to help me incorporate these stories about the skirt into a small play.

So far, I have found two young women who are willing to take on a partial sublet and a third who is currently considering. I have seen her walk by here every day and feel she would provide the skirt with its most stringent test. Attractive women attracting attractive men, well, where is the challenge for the skirt in that? But this young woman practices none of the feminine arts and, indeed, seems unaware of them. Oh, to witness when she becomes aware...

In any event, know that I am well, of good cheer and no doubt destined for greatness.

Until then, I remain, ever yours,

Franco Rossi

1

AT THE SOUND of an old-fashioned wolf whistle, Marnie LaTour looked up from her laptop, which was currently sitting on the serving counter of the Deli Dally next to her cold meatball sub. Her three co-workers from Carnahan Custom Software—all male—had swiveled on their stools to stare out the window.

"Whoa, would you look at that?" murmured one.

Marnie looked. A long-legged blonde walked by in a flippy skirt that fluttered alarmingly in the San Francisco wind. Glued to her side was one of the men from Technical Support.

"All right, Gregie boy!" Two of the guys high-fived each other.

Marnie watched long enough to see that Greg was taking the blonde to Tarantella, the new Italian restaurant down the street, then returned to the screen full of code she was trying to debug. If *she* had written the code in the first place, there wouldn't have been anything *to* debug.

"You think she's wearing a thong?" This comment came from Barry Emmons, who was sitting next to Marnie since it was his program she was trying to fix. She assumed he meant that as a rhetorical question and didn't answer.

The three men slid off the counter stools and walked over to the window.

"All I'm asking for is one really good gust of wind before they make it to the door." It was probably Doug.

"Oh, yeah." That was Barry again.

Marnie wished he'd stayed with her instead of heading for the window with the rest of them. She also wished she was dining alone with him at Tarantella instead of going with the guys to two-for-one Italian night at the Deli Dally. After all, she'd just spent three hours fixing the code for his animated oilfield tool instructional video. At least he'd bought her meatball sub.

Well, actually he'd paid for his and had given her the free one. Still. It was something. A start. And right now, Marnie needed a start.

She'd worked at Carnahan since graduating from college six years ago and had eliminated all the dating possibilities among her co-workers. Barry had been working at Carnahan less than a year and was still in the "possible" column. Word was that he'd spent time in a couple of women's "possible" columns, but wasn't dating anyone currently.

Marnie figured it was her turn, except that Barry was proving slippery to pin down. Thus, she'd volunteered her code expertise to help with his projects. Several times.

She glanced over her shoulder at the men. Clearly, he needed a nudge.

While they stood at the window, Marnie found and corrected a repeating error in a line of code. And that should do it. She brought up the animation of a rotating tool that did who-knew-what on screen and watched as it turned, opened, swiveled and let yellow arrows parade through it.

"Hey, you fixed it!" Barry and the others returned to the bar stools, the wind apparently not having cooperated.

Barry leaned one hand on the counter, blocking her from the others' sight. "You're a genius," he murmured and looked down at her, smiling.

Marnie looked up at him and her heart gave an extra blip. It was a movie moment. Inches separated their mouths and if he'd wanted to, he could have kissed her, not that he would here in the delicatessen in front of their co-workers, but still, Marnie knew they'd made a connection.

He reached in front of her and typed on her keyboard—almost suggestively—so that the program ran again. "Man, I owe you, Marnie."

She waited a beat. "Take me to Tarantella and we'll call it even."

"Tarantella." He made a rude noise. "Good one, Marnie."

"Hey, I'm serious!" She'd heard the restaurant was expensive, but it wasn't *that* expensive. She'd even order spaghetti instead of the seven-layer lasagna.

"Come on." He sat on the stool. "Tarantella is where you take your lady for a very *special*—" he raised and lowered his eyebrows "—evening."

"I happen to think three hours of my time fixing your mess is worth a special evening."

"What do you say I buy you a six-pack? You name the brand. I'll even spring for imported."

"Ooo, imported," the others mocked.

Marnie extended her hands palms up, imitating a scale. "Let's see...a six-pack of beer...dinner at Tarantella...helping Barry out of a jam...letting him spend all night trying to figure out where he screwed up in time for the client's demo tomorrow. Gee, Barry, I dunno."

"What, you want wine instead?"

There was general snickering.

Marnie glared down the bar. "No, I want dinner at Tarantella."

The others looked at each other, then stared at their plates.

"Marnie, Tarantella is a *date* restaurant. You know, it's dark, there're candles, booths, tablecloths—all that stuff. There's even a violin dude."

"Yeah, chicks love that stuff," Doug said.

Barry lowered his voice and leaned toward her. "It's where you take your *girlfriend*."

Marnie waited for Barry to connect the dots, but he was as bad at that as he was at writing code. "So?" she prompted.

He laughed as he picked up his soda. "You're not the girlfriend type."

Until a few nanoseconds ago, she'd kinda, sorta thought she was on her way to being *his* girlfriend. "What do you mean?"

Barry was still chuckling. "You know."

"Apparently I don't."

As the tone of her voice registered, Barry stopped laughing and shifted on the bar stool. Marnie was aware that the other two guys had gone very quiet.

He cleared his throat. "Well...you don't give off girlfriend vibes."

Did he really think she'd helped him because she loved extra work? And she'd just asked him to take her to a romantic restaurant. Clearly she wasn't vibe-literate. "Vibes how?"

"For one thing, you don't dress..." He made a vague gesture at her jeans and baggy sweater. He, himself, was wearing Dockers and a golf shirt with a dribble of sauce from the meatball sub. Hardly the stuff of fantasies.

Marnie thought of the blonde. "Short skirts, stiletto heels, that kind of thing?"

"Hell, yeah," Doug chimed in.

Barry made a slashing motion with his hand at others. "Not so much that, but there's a certain attitude that lets men know you're girlfriend material."

"I see." Marnie didn't like what she saw.

"Hey, don't worry about it. We like that you're one of the guys."

As if that weren't bad enough, there were murmurs of agreement from the others. Marnie just stared at him.

"It's a compliment," Barry added.

She glanced from the green awning and the liveried doorman outside Tarantella to the partially eaten, cold meatball sub next to her laptop. "It doesn't feel like a compliment."

"Trust me, it is. You're easy to work with 'cause there's none of that man/woman stuff going on."

"Oh, the available-for-sex vibes. Right."

There was not a sound in the deli.

Okay, then. Marnie saved the program to a disk which she ejected and handed to Barry.

He looked relieved. "Thanks, Marnie. You're a pal."

"Yeah, that's me. A real pal." She closed her laptop.

Barry gave her a look. "I'm telling you, you'd hate Tarantella. It's not your style."

Marnie gave him a look right back. "It could be." He wanted vibes? She'd show him vibes. One of the guys? Not anymore. Attitude? Just wait. She was going to show him so much attitude he'd *beg* her to let him take her to Tarantella. She'd make *all* of them take her to Tarantella.

Barry squinted at her before shaking his head. "I'm just not seeing it. Better take me up on the beer." He cuffed her on the shoulder. "What kind do you want?"

NOT THE GIRLFRIEND TYPE. *Vibeless. One of the guys. A pal.*

Barry had all but called her sexless. Or maybe he had. He'd definitely made it clear that she held no feminine appeal for him and, while he was at it, included the entire male gender. Even worse, the other guys hadn't contradicted him.

At this moment, Marnie wasn't too pleased with the entire male gender.

It was true that she'd prided herself on being a team player and that the guys included her in their downtime. Working with them was comfortable. She hadn't realized that it was because they'd forgotten she was a woman.

So, she'd just figure out a way to remind them.

One of the guys. Not girlfriend material.

On her way home, Marnie mentally chewed on Barry's words as she got off the bus and walked toward the 24th Street Mission BART station where she'd spend the next hour or so riding the train to Pleasant Hill, where, yes, she lived with her mother. Her mom was a great roommate—even if she weren't Marnie's mom. She did more than her share of the housework and cooking and didn't bug Marnie too much about where she was going at night...mostly because by the time Marnie got home, she was in for the evening. How exciting was that?

Yeah, now that she thought about it, that sounded like a vibeless existence. The thing was, she'd never expected that she'd end up single and still living with her mother at the age of twenty-eight. What person thinks as a kid, "I want to live at home when I grow up?" When she was young, she'd had this image of what her future would be. She couldn't exactly remember what it was, but living with her mother and sleeping in the same bedroom she'd had all her life wasn't it.

Marnie was ready to settle down, as they say. But unfortunately, she hadn't found anybody to settle with. Or even settle for.

When *was* the last time she'd been anybody's girlfriend?

Marnie stopped walking right in the middle of the sidewalk, next to a trendy boutique, one of a string of them in this block.

There had been Darren, but that hadn't lasted long and it had been the same kind of cheapie meal and occasional movie relationship she'd always had with guys. That had been fine when they were all starting out, but lately Marnie wanted more.

And, darn it, she was going to get it. Somehow.

She'd been gazing into the distance, but now she focused on the display window of the boutique. Skirts. Skimpy sweaters. Purses too tiny to be useful. Girlfriend clothes.

Marnie wore jeans and sweaters or T-shirts just like everyone else in her department. How stupid would she look if she started wearing clothes like that to work? And why should she have to change the way she dressed and fool around with her hair and makeup? She used to wear makeup, but she liked the extra sleeping time. Anyway, San Francisco's windy weather made her eyes water and the stupid mascara run, so she'd get to work and have to do everything over again. Waste of time.

And did it matter? Were men really that shallow?

Of course they were.

Grumbling to herself, Marnie rounded the corner and headed down Twenty-Third Street, her favorite part of the walk to and from the station. Her route took her past a row of Painted Ladies, the San Francisco Victorian houses. Their defiantly gaudy colors and ornate trim appealed to Marnie. Why, she didn't know. She was more of a neutral, sleek, chrome and clean lines kind of person, when she thought about decor at all. These houses were about as far from that as something could be.

This had been her route for nearly six years, uneventful until recently. First, several days ago, Marnie had noticed a sign in one of the pretty town houses—the pink-and-green one with the cream trim and darling gingerbread balcony—offering two-day rentals.

She'd memorized the sign: Two-Day Sublet. Inquire Within. There was additional writing beneath. *It is not up to me to supply reasons why you might need an apartment for two days a week. If you do, let's talk. If you do not, please walk.*

Marnie had been thinking about it—she'd even met the doorman who had insisted that she take a flyer and had talked a blue streak at her until she'd given him a politely noncommittal platitude just to get away from him. Still, it would be wonderful to avoid the tedious commute for a couple of days a week.

The other thing that had happened was that construction had begun on one of the more tawdry of the ladies across the street. The house was being completely renovated and would no doubt rent or sell to a gazillionaire, if it hadn't already.

At some point during the years since the town houses had been built in the late 1800s, they'd been updated by having their gingerbread trim torn off and new facades built over the old so that they'd lost all their personality. Now they'd get it back.

Marnie slowed to check on the progress—okay, and to see if the hunky construction foreman was around. In her current mood, Marnie could use a good construction foreman sighting.

Oh, goody. His truck was there. The blue-and-white Bronco bearing the name Renfro Restoration was parked off the sidewalk in the patch of grass by the front steps, just where it had been this morning when she'd walked by.

The guy had been solely responsible for Marnie acquiring a very expensive coffee habit. Every morning, she passed by about the time he arrived on site.

He'd lean against his Bronco and sip coffee from a familiar tall paper cup with a brown cuff around it. Though it was nearly May, the mornings were still cool and he'd wrap both hands around the cup. She could practically taste the coffee he gingerly brought to his lips. She'd think about it all the way into work and then have to stop in at the Starbucks next to the Carnahan building.

Early this morning, the two-man construction crew had been stripping the house to the insulation. Now they were cleaning up for the day. A large flatbed truck was parked on the street and the men threw the old wood and debris in it. Marnie stopped and watched them work. Actually, she watched *one* of them work because the foreman was right in there with them. His denim jacket and clipboard were on the hood of the Bronco and only a T-shirt was between him and the cooling evening.

A nicely filled out T-shirt. And jeans. Mustn't overlook the jeans that emphasized a flat, taut stomach that clearly didn't have a cold meatball sub sitting in it.

A broken two-by-four hit the side of the truck, bounced off and landed near Marnie. Startled, she jumped.

"Watch it!" The foreman approached her and Marnie's eyes widened.

He was so much...*more* up close. Muscles and sinews worked in perfect rhythm as he strode toward her. Sawdust and other bits of old house dusted his shoulders and clung to his hair. Testosterone clouded the air. Everything about him shouted *I am man and I do manly things.* And the subtext which was, of course, *I demand a woman who does womanly things.*

Marnie doubted writing computer code counted as a womanly thing, but was willing to try to convince him.

He came to a stop in front of her, his shortish sun-kissed hair ruffling attractively in the wind. He wore gloves and swiped the back of his wrist over his forehead before resting his hands at his waist. His stance indicated that he was used to being in charge.

Marnie sighed a little. He could be in charge of her any time.

"You okay?" he asked.

She managed to nod. This was a lot of man and she wasn't exactly sure what to do.

Apparently she didn't have to do anything. He picked up the board and tossed it into the truck bed. "It's dangerous to stand this close." Then he walked back to the pile and picked up more wood. He raised his eyebrows until Marnie realized he was waiting for her to move on.

Way to go, Marnie. Talk about vibeless.

Couldn't she have managed to come up with something to say? One measly conversational opener? She worked with men all day long and she couldn't figure out an approach?

Talk about seriously rusty. The fact that he was a

completely different type for her was no excuse. So his in-your-face masculinity had rendered her mute. Clearly, she needed help.

Disgusted with herself, she hunched into her ski parka and buried her nose in her woolen scarf as the wind picked up. Where was spring already?

She crossed the street, which brought her right by the Victorian with the two-day rent sign in the window. But she wasn't looking at the sign—she was using the window's reflection to watch the construction guy some more.

That was one serious hunk of man.

And she hadn't even pinged his radar.

But to be fair, guys like that had never pinged her radar, either. She'd always gone for cerebral types, and the foreman was more the "hunka hunka burnin' luv" type.

As Marnie stood there thinking that maybe the cerebral types she knew could use a testosterone transfusion, the door to the Victorian opened and two tiny, long-haired dogs—the kind that barked in annoying little yips—led a tall, thin man down the steps. The doorman.

"Slow down or you'll strangle yourselves, you irritating little twits."

The dogs ignored him and struggled to descend the stairs. Once down on the sidewalk, they sniffed at Marnie's shoes.

The doorman pulled at the leash. "I'd say heel, but they'd only think I was suggesting another part of your foot." He looked up at her. "Oh, it's you. Have you decided about the apartment?"

"Uh..." Marnie stepped back and the dogs yipped in protest. "I was just..." She trailed off.

Wait a minute. She was just having a pity party because Barry had rejected her and she'd been thrown for a loop by the construction guy.

She needed to make some changes and here was an opportunity being handed to her. Just because it was attached to a couple of high-strung dogs shouldn't distract her.

The bottom line was that she wanted a boyfriend. A serious boyfriend. A potential husband boyfriend. There was even a technical name for that—fiancé. With her commute, it was hard to date either in the city or in Pleasant Hill. Renting this apartment would give her a temporary base in the city.

She'd just about decided when the sound of gears grinding announced the imminent departure of the flatbed truck. The construction foreman was still there sweeping leftover debris off the sidewalk.

Oh, yes. And as an added perk, she'd wake up to him outside her window.

Marnie looked back at the doorman, who'd been remarkably patient when she sensed that he wasn't the patient type.

"Yes, I'd like to rent the apartment for two days a week." It was the first impulsive thing she'd ever done.

He pulled on the dogs' leashes. "Monday and Tuesday is all that I have left."

Those weren't date nights. "Monday and Tuesday will be fine." She'd make them date nights.

"Fabulous! But as you see, I am otherwise engaged. When can you come by to do the paperwork?"

"Tomorrow morning?" Marnie still couldn't believe what she'd done.

"How do you take your coffee?"

Marnie blinked at the question. "Large and strong." Kinda like the construction guy. She almost giggled.

"Understood. Until tomorrow then. Onward, dogs!" The doorman proceeded up the street, fortunately in the opposite direction.

Okay. She'd done it. Now how was she going to tell her mother that she'd rented an apartment in the city for two days a week? Marnie started walking when a whistle pierced the air. Not from the man with the dogs, but from the crew in the truck.

Instinctively, Marnie knew it was a different whistle than the ones the construction workers used to signal each other. Glancing across the street, she saw two women walking, heads bowed against the wind just as hers was when she walked.

That was the only similarity. Where Marnie was dressed in clunky hiking boots, jeans and appropriately warm clothing for a San Francisco spring evening, these stupid females were wearing heels and skirts which blew every which way as their long blond hair whipped about their faces.

What was this? Blonde Day? And why were they all dressed alike?

The wind carried the murmur of appreciative males. The construction workers, clearly unrepentant, had whistled at the women and now watched as they walked past the truck. Ah yes, the call of the male *hominus jerkus.*

They hadn't whistled at *her,* not that she'd ever had a construction worker whistle at her or wanted one to. Or was supposed to want one to.

And yet, and yet... No. If that was what she had to wear to get whistled at, then forget it.

She stood and watched the men watching the women.

"Hey! Haul that stuff off to the dump!" The foreman glanced at the women then tossed a bag of sweepings into the back of the truck. It drove away and the foreman walked into the yard where he set up two sawhorses and a work light clipped to the open door of the Bronco.

He was still in his T-shirt, impervious to the cold. The muscles in his back stretched, the muscles in his arms bunched and his torso was probably a work of art.

Marnie sighed. If she were going to have a man whistle at her, that was the one she wanted doing the whistling.

But he hadn't even acknowledged her presence.

She should get going or she'd miss her usual train. Except something drew her to the man in the yard. Marnie stepped off the curb and crossed the street. What would she do if he did notice her?

Put out some vibes, that's what.

The whine of an electric saw shrieked into the evening. Marnie made the brilliant deduction that he was cutting a piece of wood. He wore safety goggles and looked solid and competent and was concentrating as fiercely on the movements of the saw as Marnie usually did staring at a computer screen. Of course if Marnie made a mistake, she wasn't likely to lose a finger.

A man at work was a thing of beauty. If that wasn't a famous quote, it should be. Yeah, if nothing else, seeing more of this guy made renting the apartment worth it.

Knowing that he couldn't hear her, Marnie shouted, "You're a thing of beauty! And I just rented the apartment across the street. What do you think of that?"

The saw reached the end of the board. The whine stopped and a chunk of wood fell to the ground. Setting the saw aside, the man picked up the part he'd cut and held it to the light. As he examined his work and blew bits of shaving and sawdust off the design, a huge smile creased his face.

ZACH RENFRO liked nothing more than restoring San Francisco's grand Victorians. He did excellent work, if he did say so himself. No one could afford him, but since he didn't charge what he was worth, it all evened out.

People lacked patience these days. People like the actor type who lived in the Victorian across the street. The day Zach and his crew had started ripping off the disgusting dress this pretty lady had worn for the past seventy-five years, the guy had swished across the street to complain about the noise. He'd blathered on about a script and how Zach was committing auditory assault.

"What the hell are you talking about?" Zach had

climbed down a ladder to talk with the guy and wasn't pleased about the interruption.

"I have work to do. How can I concentrate with all this commotion?"

"Earplugs?"

"I, Franco Rossi, should not have to wear earplugs in the privacy of my own home." He gave Zach a haughty look.

Great. One of those. "Well, Frank." Zach couldn't believe anyone would admit to being named Franco and shortened it out of courtesy. "This is my work."

"But *my* work is art."

Zach gestured to the house. "So is mine. Once upon a time, my lady, here, was just as pretty as your house. But she wasn't treated right and now I'm going to give her a little nip and tuck, get her a new dress and make her a pretty necklace." Zach reached into the front seat of his truck and grabbed the piece of wood that he planned to use as a pattern to cut gingerbread trim. "Now look at that. It's a custom design and I'm going to cut it out by hand. Are you going to tell me that's not art?"

Franco stared at the wood, then raised one well-shaped—probably plucked—eyebrow. "My apologies for not recognizing a fellow artiste." He bowed. *Bowed.* Zach glanced around to see if his crew noticed.

"So you will understand if I confess that the call of my muse is so faint that your muse is drowning her out."

"Hang on." Zach bent down and rummaged in the open toolbox propped on the front steps. Inside was a package of earplugs. He shook out a couple and handed them to Frank. "Occasionally, my muse gets loud even for me."

Franco stared at the two pieces of bright yellow foam. "Do you have these in blue?"

"No."

He sighed, then pasted a brave smile on his face. "I shall persevere."

Zach hadn't seen him since. Fortunately.

He liked working in this area of San Francisco. There was a lot of contrast with the edge of the Mission District and the trendy part of Valencia Street. He wouldn't mind living in a place like this. Of course, he wouldn't mind living in any of the Victorians he'd restored. That was the secret to his inspiration—he got emotionally involved in them. It wasn't practical, but he left the practical part of running Renfro Construction to his father and his brother, who had enough practicality to spare. Enough for Zach to be Renfro Restoration. So what if he did get a few pangs at the end of a project? Another one always came along.

Zach took a deep breath of the cool evening air and turned on the saw. The drone of the blade as it cut through the wood served as a soothing backdrop for his thoughts.

In spite of all evidence to the contrary, there was a practical side to Zach and that practical side, a residual of years working in the office side of the business, pointed out that there were thousands of very good commercial patterns and manufacturers of Victorian gingerbread trims. And even if he wanted to continue to provide custom designs, he could recycle his more successful ones to increase the profit margin. It would still be a Renfro Restoration original, but he could outsource the fabrication and carry the designs in stock. Construction time and standby labor time would be less, thus increasing the profit margin.

Lord knew it wouldn't take much to increase the profit margin. But knowing each house was unique appealed to Zach's pride and an artistic sense he hadn't known he had.

He owed his father and brother big-time for letting him run this part of the company. They never said a word when Zach's penchant for perfectionism ate into the already slim profits.

And he was just so much happier doing this than anything else. They knew that, too.

So, he'd work on this new trim design tonight so he wouldn't have to pay standby time to the crew tomorrow.

Zach concentrated on working the jigsaw and holding the wood steady. One slip would ruin the design. Yeah, there were nails and wood glue, but that was a last resort.

He became aware of a blob of bright colors in his peripheral vision. The blob could have been there any number of minutes since his vision was partially blocked by the side of the safely glasses. He'd seen that blob before—walking by every day and a little while ago it had nearly been beaned with a piece of wood.

Without turning his head, Zach swiveled his eyes. Gotta be a homeless person wandering the streets—the giant ski parka, jeans, well-worn boots, the bag, the wool hat pulled over his...her? ears, but especially the way he/she stood there and talked to him or herself.

The guy was probably going to sleep in the house once Zach left. At this stage in the construction, Zach didn't particularly mind, but in a couple of days, he was going to have to secure the place to protect the remodeling and tools from vandals.

But right now, he needed to concentrate on working with a lethally sharp saw.

MARNIE SHOVED her hands into her pockets as she watched the man work. His corded muscles were nicely defined by the T-shirt. His jeans did some nice defining, too. Very nice.

Surprisingly nice. Marnie wasn't in the habit of noticing nice things like that. Hmm. This was a habit she should cultivate. What kind of trance had she been in the past few years? Oh, Barry had been nice looking in his own way but there was something about this guy...something elemental and real—talk about projecting, but who cared?—that appealed to Marnie.

What type of girlfriend would a man like that want?

Emboldened by the concealing whine of the saw, Marnie decided to ask him. "Hey, you. Yeah, you—big, strong, musclely construction guy. So what's a girl gotta do to be *your* girlfriend?"

The pitch of the whine lowered as the saw bit into the wood. Marnie admired the shape of the man's arms. A girl generally didn't see arms like that in the computer field.

"You're probably the short, tight skirt, big hair and makeup sort, aren't cha, Big Guy?"

Big Guy responded by turning so Marnie had a better view of his chest. "Whoo-hoo! You know, for you, it might be worth it. A girl could get lost in those arms. And I'll bet you'd never ask your girlfriend to paint or pound nails and then buy her a lousy sandwich. You're probably a simple man with simple needs."

Marnie suddenly had some of those same needs. What a coincidence. She and the construction guy had something in common. She could work with common needs.

"And I bet you don't have a whole lot of brains to get in the way of those needs, do you? Nope. Not you. But you know what I'm thinking? I'm thinking brains are overrated. Men with brains just think about the same things anyway, so what do they need brains for?"

Marnie shifted her bag to her other shoulder and shoved her hands back into her pockets. She should get going, but it felt good to shout out her frustrations with the male population to an actual man. The fact that he wasn't Barry and couldn't hear didn't matter at all.

"Yeah, you're just the kind of guy I could go for, if only...if only you'd turn around so I could see whether or not you've got a cute butt."

There was silence. An all-encompassing silence. A silence that had begun midway through her last sentence. A silence into which the words "you've got a cute butt" rang out clearly. Irrevocably.

Humiliatingly.

She should run. Fast. Now.

She should, but she didn't.

The construction foreman, aka Big Guy, pulled off the clear safety goggles as he straightened and ran his fingers through sunstreaked hair. He gave her a cocky grin. "Thanks."

Marnie's face was so hot, she was surprised little clouds of steam weren't rising from her cheeks. "I was just—I didn't say—there was more to the sentence!"

"How much more?"

"What I said was, I *wished* you'd turn around so I...could tell..." Not helping. Not helping.

He inclined his head and obligingly turned around.

Oh. My. Gosh. First of all, he *actually* turned around. Second, he really *did* have a cute butt.

Now what was she supposed to do? Because eventually, Marnie knew he would turn back—the way he was this very second—and she would be expected to say something. Under the circumstances, she supposed witty and profound was out.

"Well?" he prompted. He had just the sort of voice she expected a manly man—and what was construction work if not manly?—would have.

Marnie swallowed. "Very nice, thank you."

"Nice?"

She nodded.

"Not cute?"

"Oh! Yes! Yes, of course it's cute." She was not having this conversation. She simply was not. This was an alternate universe and the construction worker with the cute butt was just a figment of her imagination.

A figment that was walking over to the sidewalk. She should say something that didn't involve body parts. "You're doing great on the house."

What a wonderfully insightful remark. So far, he'd torn everything off the front, so who knew if he was doing a good job or not?

"Thanks." He came to a stop a careful distance away from her and proceeded to subject her to an unabashedly thorough scrutiny. His gaze flicked over her hat, dwelt on her face and lingered questioningly on her puffy ski parka. Then, of all things, he studied her shoes and narrowed his eyes on the black canvas pouch containing her laptop. It wasn't a normal laptop case because Marnie didn't particularly want to advertise that she was carrying an expensive piece of computer equipment when she walked through the neighborhood.

Now, the man couldn't expect to stare at her like that without being stared at in return, and Marnie figured she might as well stare since she'd already blown the first impression. She truly wasn't the sort to make lewd remarks at construction workers.

At least she hadn't been a couple of days ago.

Marnie wished that he'd say something. She wasn't ready to try her luck again at meaningful conversation.

He drew his hands to his waist and regarded her sympathetically. "You need a place to stay tonight?"

Marnie nearly swallowed her tongue. "I—" Apparently it was very easy to become this type of man's girlfriend. Too easy.

"You hungry?" He used his teeth to pull off this work glove, dug in his back pocket and withdrew his wallet.

He was going to offer her money.

She took a step backward. "I—I'm fine. I live with my mom in Pleasant Hill." That sounded very sophisticated. "I'm headed to the 24th Street Mission station." Continuing to back away from him, she hooked a thumb over her shoulder. "It's just a couple of blocks this way. I should get going." Giving him a quick nod, Marnie decisively strode toward the BART terminal. She was walking uphill and her shins began to tingle, but she wasn't going to slow down.

And she wasn't going to look back, either.

2

The Legend of The Skirt

by Franco Rossi

Act One, Scene One.

Exterior: Charming Victorian

Camera pans (unless is play) details of Victorian woodwork.

ENTER: (unless is movie, then camera zooms in through window) Handsome, with an air of superiority that he tries to hide, charismatic doorman, clearly bound for greater things.

(Note to self: decide if writing a play or movie)

A Skirt in San Francisco
A Play in Three Acts
by Franco Rossi

Act One, Scene One.

A world-renowned parapsychologist, acting as a doorman, (see above description) successfully rents his apartment to three women who will time-share during the week. The possessor of a skirt, which, legend has it, attracts men (and he must rely on legend since he is immune to the skirt), he awaits the opportunity to study the skirt's effects firsthand.

(Note to self: keep it snappy, keep it moving)

Ms. Monday-Tuesday is a preoccupied computer programmer. Very smart, but very unaware. Nice eyes and hair—needs a trim—has no clue how to dress, presumably a good figure, but how would one know beneath the sleeping bag she wears as a coat? Wants to give city living a try and a break from long commute.

Ms. Wednesday-Thursday is looking for her father. Something mysterious going on there. Must explore.

Sadly, Ms. Friday-Saturday used to own the apartment and is attempting to get on with her life after a broken engagement.

(Note to self: take notes before writing script.)

(Additional note to self: Wear earplugs only if sitting in foyer, otherwise cannot hear doorbell.)

IT HAD BEEN several days since Zach had seen the homeless person. He hadn't meant to scare her—he'd decided the person was a "her"—but that might be the best thing if it had sent her on home. These runaways took to the streets thinking it was a solution to their problems. Maybe in some cases it was, but that kid was too soft for that kind of life.

And then this morning, there she was again, dragging her belongings behind her. She hadn't had the duffel when he'd seen her last week. He wondered if she'd stolen it or accepted a handout from somebody.

Surreptitiously from his perch on the ladder, Zach watched her climb the steps to a Victorian across the street and was more than surprised when that Frank character opened the door and let her in. Moments later, without the duffel, she climbed down the steps and hurried on up the street.

Zach started down the ladder, intending to check on the guy, but stopped. It wasn't any of his business. Besides, Frank came and went all the time. If Zach didn't see him by noon, he'd check up on him then.

In the meantime, he had some trim to finish tacking up.

Man, he loved his job. Even when things went wrong, he loved his work.

Zach had cut out thirty-six linear feet of gingerbread trim. This morning, he was tacking it between the bay window on the ground floor and the upper floor bay window, the oriel, to see how it looked.

It was an ornate pattern, full of curves and swoops and intricate cutouts because Zach wanted to show off a little bit. He hammered up the three strips, then climbed down the ladder and walked to the edge of the front yard.

An excellent job, if he did say so himself. But the trim didn't have the impact he'd thought it would. He tried to imagine various exterior color schemes that would highlight the pattern, but the problem was that the curves and cutouts and curlicues were too small for the scale. The intricacies of the design were lost. Maybe if he painted the house a dark color and the gingerbread white, like icing, it would work.

He was standing there imagining it when he heard a throat clear behind him and was relieved to see Franco from across the street. He was walking three dogs, yet managed the leashes in a way that told Zach he'd done it many times before.

"Would you be adverse to a comment from a layman?"

"Go for it."

"The trim doesn't work."

Zach exhaled heavily. "I know."

"It's too fussy."

"I prefer ornate."

"I prefer ornate, too, but sometimes, less is more, if you know what I mean."

Zach had meant the *word* "ornate," but he let it pass.

Franco shifted the leashes to one hand and gestured up and down. "Look at the tailored lines of the house."

Zach knew what he meant. "It's Sticks-Eastlake style. See the square bay window? And there are still some of the original wooden strips outlining it." Restoration was Zach's favorite subject. "When the facade is finished, there will be more strips outlining the doors and the framework of the house and then—"

Franco held up a hand. "My point is that you wouldn't dress a gloriously statuesque six-foot tall woman in girlish frills and lace, would you?"

"A gloriously statuesque six-foot tall woman can wear whatever the hell she wants."

"No, she can't." Franco was firm on this. "She can wear the clean, dramatic lines and bold patterns and color that would overwhelm a more petite woman. Likewise, your house. Enhance. Do not detract."

As Franco babbled about Amazons, Zach immediately saw why his previous design hadn't worked. His curls and curves fought with the clean lines of the house. This particular style of Victorian was known for gingerbread embellishment, but clearly, it had to be the right gingerbread.

Franco had moved on to domes and turrets, equating them with hats and turbans. Zach wasn't going in that direction, but he did have another idea for a gingerbread pattern with straight lines and spare curves.

"You've got a good eye," he said to Franco.

"Yes. And I'm especially good with colors, should you find yourself in need of a second opinion."

In spite of himself, Zach felt the edges of his mouth turn up. "I'll keep that in mind. Hey, have you seen that homeless girl around here?"

"One sees so many."

"I'm talking about the one you let in this morning."

Franco's face was blank.

"Giant coat? Funky hat? I know, that sounds like most of them."

"Ah." Franco raised his finger. "I know who you mean. She's not homeless."

Zach exhaled. "Good to hear. I thought she looked a little soft for the streets."

"Not to worry."

Franco and the dogs walked on and Zach got to work designing a crenelated running trim with wagon wheel spokes that would be a bear to cut out. But worth it.

OKAY. HERE IT WAS. Marnie's first night in the Victorian apartment.

"Welcome, welcome." Franco, her new landlord,

bowed and ushered her into a jungle. *"Mi casa es su casa."*

"At least on Mondays and Tuesdays," Marnie said. "What's with the greenery?"

"I'm plant sitting." He gave her a sly look. "Normally, I would put them on my balcony, but I didn't want to intrude."

Marnie knew a hint when she heard one. "I don't care if you put the plants on the balcony. I like plants."

"Excellent." Franco handed her a huge Boston fern. "Go on. I'll be right behind you."

Marnie could hardly see around the plant, but climbed the stairs to the second-floor apartment, 2B.

There were four apartments in the old Victorian, but she gathered that Franco was the only one renting his out piecemeal.

She thought it was clever of him, actually. This way, he could concentrate on his script. And he was, no doubt, making more money than if he'd rented it to one person. And, as he had told her, Sundays were his.

Franco had given her a key when she'd dropped off her suitcase and duffel this morning and now Marnie unlocked the door and stepped inside. She set the fern down by the front door and surveyed the apartment.

It was exquisitely decorated in period furniture that made Marnie nervous, but she figured she'd either get used to it or break something. Probably both. She immediately went over to the bay window, from which she could see the work going on across the street and looked for the construction guy.

He wasn't there. She was relieved in a way, but

knew that she'd have to speak to him again at some point. They were pseudo-neighbors now, after all.

It was only hours after their evening encounter last week that Marnie had realized that the man hadn't been hitting on her. He'd been offering her help. It said a lot about him and unfortunately, something about her as well.

Girlfriend material. As if. She cringed inwardly and it was a feeling she was getting tired of.

A great huffing and puffing announced Franco's arrival. He'd rigged a pole to hold several hanging baskets and looked like an ancient Chinese water bearer.

"I'm not doing that again!" he moaned. "We'll just have to make more trips."

Marnie heard the "we'll," but figured she'd let him get away with it this time.

Franco staggered into the bedroom. "Hurry, hurry."

Marnie followed him and opened the French doors to the balcony.

With much moaning and groaning, Franco knelt and raised the pole.

Marnie helped him get the hanging baskets off. She watched as he arranged them on a pretty white wrought iron plant tree, then brought him the giant fern.

"That, we'll put in the corner. All right, then. Next load."

Marnie didn't mind helping since she hadn't actually thought about what she would do tonight. She hadn't eaten and she wanted to get settled in, then maybe explore the neighborhood streets she didn't see every morning on her walk.

Franco had allocated part of the bedroom closet to her and she understood that the other tenants of 2B would also have closet privileges. Not that she planned to leave much stuff here, but it was nice to know that she didn't have to lug everything with her each week.

After she and Franco had brought up the rest of the plants, he offered her tea.

"That sounds good."

"I left a few basics in the kitchen and you're welcome to help yourself. I suppose you and the others can use boxes or labeling to keep your things straight." Franco put water on to boil and gave her a tour of the kitchen amenities at the same time.

Marveling at the novelty of having a man wait on her, Marnie shrugged off her parka and sat at the kitchen table. Franco leaned against the counter as he waited for the water to boil.

"And now you must tell me everything about yourself."

"I gave you my social security number. My life is now an open book."

"I'm talking about more than good credit and your employment history. I want to know about a woman with the unusual name of Marnie LaTour, her hopes and dreams—and how she believes renting an apartment for two days a week will help her achieve them."

Well, put that way...one second she was staring into the friendly, but inquisitive, eyes of her landlord/

doorman and the next moment, Marnie had burst into tears.

Marnie couldn't remember the last time she'd cried. Long, long, ago. She supposed that since her father had died right after she got out of college, she hadn't had much to cry about. She had a good job, friends and the San Francisco public transportation system. What was there to cry about?

This was so embarrassing. "I'm s-sorry."

Franco calmly went about the task of making tea. "I find myself confronted by crying women on a fairly regular basis."

"I don't even know why I'm crying," Marnie wailed.

"Yes, you do. You just aren't ready to tell me about it." A cup of hot tea appeared in front of her, along with a tissue, which she accepted gratefully.

"It's so stupid," she mumbled, holding the tissue against her nose.

"Not if it makes you cry."

"Crying's stupid, too."

Franco sipped his tea and said nothing.

Eventually, Marnie couldn't stand the sound of her sniffing in the silence and blurted out, "It's just that a man at work, someone I thought I liked, told me I wasn't girlfriend material, which I knew because the construction workers never whistle at me and I don't even know why I care."

She sniffed. Again.

Franco clasped his hands together. "May I take notes?"

"Why?"

"I'm a student of the human condition and hope to incorporate certain stories into my scripts."

Great. She was a human condition. Marnie held her head in her hands. "I don't care."

"Does it matter if it becomes a film script?"

Like it would ever be produced. "No."

Franco went to the telephone table and returned with a pen and pad of paper and began scribbling. "Now what else is bothering you?"

"My mother is going to Paris," Marnie threw in for good measure. She'd just found out.

Franco gasped. "And not taking you?"

"She's chaperoning the French club. She teaches high school."

Franco gestured dismissively. "Consider yourself lucky, then. You don't want Paris at this time of year. Now, what do you want?" He stared at the pad of paper. "Do I understand that you wish construction workers to objectify you?"

"No! Well, kinda... Actually, I guess I just want to be the sort of woman they would want to objectify—whistle at. You know."

"I'm getting the idea, but please enlighten me."

And so Marnie told him all about Barry and not being girlfriend material and the construction workers and the foreman thinking she was a homeless person. Franco nodded and said "Uh-huh" and "mmm" a lot as he took notes.

He was such a good listener that Marnie even told him how she'd worried about telling her mother she'd be staying here and how her mother had misunderstood and thought she was moving out and that her mom had been so happy that now Marnie was really going to have to look for somewhere else to live. None of this had anything to do with being girlfriend material, but Marnie had thought she was helping her mother by living with her and now her mother didn't need help anymore and it was Just One More Thing.

"I'm sorry to be such a drama queen," she moaned, holding her head.

"Drama is my life," Franco said fervently. "What are you going to do?"

Marnie drank her entire mug of lukewarm tea. "I don't know."

"Yes, you do." Franco tapped his pencil impatiently.

She did know. "Okay, but I don't know how."

"Oh, hon, you don't want that Barry creature."

"Oh, no. But I want him to ask me out to Tarantella. I want him to beg me."

"And you want the construction workers to whistle at you."

"Maybe just once."

"I could pay them for you."

Marnie laughed, then immediately sobered. "You're saying that's the only way—"

"No, it was a joke. A bad one. But I did make you laugh." He studied her and Marnie was reminded of the construction foreman's thorough scrutiny.

"We have a lot of work ahead of us." Franco stood.

"We?"

"You didn't think I wouldn't respond to your cry for help, did you? We'll start by doing your colors."

"What?"

"We'll ascertain which colors are most flattering to you before we go shopping, my little Cinderella."

"*Shopping* isn't one of my favorite words. I mostly order online."

Franco gave a world-weary sigh. He used sighs very effectively. "I shall return with my swatches. You need to change."

"I know."

"I meant your clothes. What did you bring?"

Marnie looked down at herself. "Uh, more jeans. Some T-shirts."

"Do you have a white T-shirt?"

"Mostly white. It's got the blue writing on it from the Carnahan Easter 10K Fun Run."

"Wear it backward or turn it inside out. And let me check my costumes—"

"You have costumes?"

"Yes, I'm an actor and a playwright and sometimes due to budgetary constraints in the small theaters, one must exercise many talents." He headed for the door. "I'll be back."

Marnie cleared away the teacups and unpacked her suitcase. The closet was empty, except for a large hanging bag. She hung up three T-shirts, two pairs of jeans and her pajamas and robe. She didn't know what to do with her underwear, so she left it in the duffel, which she set on the closet floor.

"Yoo-hoo," she heard. Marnie couldn't remember a time when she'd ever heard a grown man say "Yoo-hoo."

Franco was in the living room. He'd pulled a chair over to the bay window and had taken the shade off the lamps, which he'd turned on. "We'll need to see how you look in both natural and artificial light."

Marnie pictured the Carnahan offices. "I spend most of my day in fluorescent light."

"How ghastly." Franco grimaced. "I found a nice, plain, black skirt I think will fit you. Go put it on."

"A skirt? Isn't denim a neutral color?"

Franco pinched the top of his nose and inhaled. "Marnie, please start thinking outside the box."

Apparently thinking outside the box meant putting on the black skirt. Fine. Whatever.

Marnie already had on the white T-shirt and now she added the skirt. It slipped smoothly over her head and settled around her hips, swirling around her thighs before brushing its hem around midknee.

Marnie couldn't remember the last time she'd worn a skirt or a dress and yet she'd been faithfully shaving her legs just the same. Now was the payoff. Who would have known?

She zipped up the skirt and looked at her reflection in the full-length mirror on the closet door. Even she, fashion nihilist that she was, could see that the black skirt was probably the most flattering thing she'd ever worn. And it fit. Maybe a little loose at the waist, but that was just lasagna-eating room.

She smoothed her palms against the material noting the thick, rich feel. She turned to the side and thought for a moment that she saw a glimmer, but when she looked closer, it was gone.

What material was this? Some kind of silk, she guessed. Good quality stuff.

"Marnie? Are you about ready, hon?"

"Coming." With a last look at herself, she headed for the door, the skirt warmly caressing her legs as she walked. She'd taken off her hiking boots and was walking barefoot across the wooden floor. The skirt made her walk differently. She could feel it in the sway of her hips and the placement of her feet and caught herself emphasizing certain movements in order to feel the material of the skirt against her skin.

She could be on to something here.

"Come, come." Franco gestured impatiently. "And let down the hair—oh those ends...well, baby steps...baby steps."

Marnie took a seat in front of the window and for the next few hours—actually only about thirty minutes—Franco draped scarves next to her face and made her look into a hand mirror. There were three piles of scarves: those that made something about her "pop," which she learned was a good thing, and those that made her look like a corpse, which was a bad thing. Then there was the secondary pile, the "only if it's on sale" pile.

She was gratified that the colors in her parka made the pop pile, but Franco only shook his head. "Colors aren't everything. However, you lucky, lucky girl, you're a Deep Autumn. You can wear black."

"Everyone can wear black."

"Everyone does wear black, but not everyone should."

Franco gathered up his scarves then presented her with a swatch sampler. "You may borrow this if you swear that you'll use it. Also, I will give you a list of acceptable boutiques where you may shop and put your choices on hold. I'll stop by and approve them and you can make the final purchase then."

The nerve of him! Marnie did not remember agreeing to any of this: Franco approving her clothes, making her take swatches, for heaven's sake. She hardly knew him. Marnie opened her mouth, then closed it. Franco seemed to be awfully sure of himself. And she wasn't.

Marnie smoothed the skirt over her lap and remembered the way it made her feel as she walked across the room. Okay, so what was the harm in buying a few new clothes? She knew she was going to have to change her appearance and if she didn't find anything she liked, no one was going to force her to buy it.

She gave Franco a sideways glance. Well, he just might. He handed her the swatch cards. "Thanks, Franco," she said meekly.

Franco snapped his scarf case shut. "I have some errands to run, but in about half an hour, I'm going to Tony's grocery. You can come with me, if you like, and I'll introduce you to Tony."

"Thanks, Franco, I would."

Amazing how some silly scarves and an offer to go to the grocery store could improve her mood, but it did. Being with Franco was going to be fun.

Marnie went into the bedroom, strangely loathe to take off the skirt. She was standing in front of the mirror turning this way and that when she heard a crash from the balcony.

One of the plants. It had to be. She just hoped it wasn't the whole plant stand.

The evening breeze had picked up and Marnie was

chilled as she opened the French doors and stepped out onto the balcony. The giant fern had blown over. It needed a bigger pot to make it more stable, though Marnie guessed that when it was hanging, it didn't matter.

She knelt and scooped up the dirt that had spilled out of the pot. A gust of wind swirled around the tiny balcony sending the hem of her skirt rippling way up her thighs and making her flash anyone who happened to be walking along the sidewalk—or renovating a house across the street. Marnie grabbed the skirt and the fern tipped over again.

There were tricks to wearing a skirt that she'd forgotten. She darted a quick look across the street but, thankfully, didn't see anyone. The Bronco was there, so she knew the construction guy was around somewhere. Marnie cleaned up the dirt again and hooked the big fern around the balcony railing. It rolled from side to side a little, but that was better than tipping over.

Marnie stood. While she was out here, she ought to check the plant stand.

The pots were swaying, but Franco had wedged the heavy stand in a corner. Just to make sure, Marnie moved one of the matching wrought iron chairs from the little table set next to the stand.

The chair had chipped white paint and bits of rust on the seat. It looked extremely uncomfortable. Marnie couldn't imagine anyone—even Franco—sitting in it, but from the street, the tableau probably looked very picturesque.

Another gust of wind caught her skirt and slammed

the glass door shut so hard, the pane rattled. Moist San Francisco night air misted Marnie's thighs before she could yank the skirt back down.

Good grief! The whole block had probably seen her underwear by now. Holding the skirt in place with one hand, Marnie tried to open the French door with the other.

It was locked.

She rattled the handle. She tried pulling up and turning. She tried pushing down and turning. She tried kicking, but since she was barefoot it hurt her more than the door.

Great. Now what? She could break the glass and unlock the door, assuming the lock wasn't broken, which she suspected it was. Or she could try to get Franco's attention.

Marnie leaned over the balcony. "Franco! Franco, can you hear me?" The front door was just beneath her.

There was no answer and Marnie remembered that Franco had said something about running errands. He'd also said something about returning in half an hour.

Okay, then. She'd give him half an hour and then she'd break the glass.

Or she'd give him until her feet went numb, whichever came first.

3

M. IS IN THE SKIRT. *It was almost too easy. Of course, I shall tell her nothing of its special properties.*

It had better find someone worthy of her. We'll be going out later for a test spin.

ZACH DIDN'T KNOW why he chose that moment to go outside, but he was glad he did. Otherwise, he wouldn't have noticed the pretty brunette on the balcony across the street.

Where had she come from? After three weeks on the site, Zach had learned the rhythm of the street and recognized most of the inhabitants, but he didn't recognize her and even at this distance, she wasn't the sort of woman a man forgot.

Speaking of forgetting, Zach couldn't remember why he'd come outside. All he'd done was stare at her as she sat in a chair and looked up and down the street.

There wasn't much going on and not too many people were out. Most were on their way home from work or having dinner.

Zach stood in the front doorway and watched her grab at her skirt, fighting with the wind. She was cold, because she kept rubbing her arms and he wasn't sure, but he thought she might be barefoot.

Why didn't she go inside if she was cold?

She stood and stomped around the balcony then walked over to the door and stared at it, rattled the handle, then looked around the balcony before picking up one of the prissy chairs.

As she took a step backward, a thought whispered through his mind. *She's going to break the glass.*

"Wait! That glass might be original to the house!" He started running across the street. "Hey, wait!"

She heard him and set the chair down just as he squeezed through cars parked bumper to bumper along the curb and stopped beneath the balcony.

"You weren't going to break the door, were you?" he called.

She came to the edge of the balcony. "That was the idea."

"Why?"

"Because I'm locked out. Because I am very cold and I can't climb down and jumping would be stupid, even if my feet *are* numb." She spoke slowly, as though he had no brains, but since all he was doing was staring at her and watching her mouth move, she might be justified in that assumption.

He liked watching her mouth move. She had a great mouth, even if it was a little on the blue side.

Though he should probably help her get inside, there was just something about her that kept Zach staring at her. Her hair was blowing every which way, which clearly annoyed her, but every time she pushed a piece out of her face, her skirt blew around. That annoyed, her, too.

It didn't annoy Zach, at all. He'd caught several glimpses of a fine set of legs that went with a fine set of everything else, as far as he could see.

She gave him an annoyed look and grabbed the chair again. "You might want to stand out of the way. I wouldn't want you to get hit by flying glass or anything."

Zach gave himself a mental shake. "Hang on and let me get a ladder."

As he bounded back across the street, he had one goal and one goal only: to get closer to the woman on the balcony.

Talk about being hit hard. Five minutes ago, he'd been completely unaware of her existence. Now she was all he could think about. Making sure he had a small set of screwdrivers, Zach carried an aluminum extension ladder back across the street. Propping it against the balcony, he climbed toward the dark-haired woman.

Her arms were crossed in front of her and she shivered as he swung a leg over the balcony and tried to find a place to stand that wasn't covered in plants.

"Here." She pulled a pot out of the way and shivered again.

Zach immediately took off his denim jacket and draped it around her shoulders, his hands lingering a moment on her arms.

She looked startled before giving him a grateful smile. "It's warm." She hugged the jacket to her.

Zach didn't notice the cold. It could have been

snowing and he wouldn't have noticed. An earthquake and he wouldn't have noticed. He was having his own private earthquake, thank you very much. Who was she and why did he care so much?

He wanted to enfold her in his arms and hold her until she stopped shivering. And then he'd hold her some more. What was it about her that made him feel this way? He didn't even know her.

"You're staring at me."

"I...was thinking that you looked good in the jacket."

She looked down at herself. "Do I? Ha. I knew denim was a neutral."

Zach had no idea what she meant and didn't care. "What's your name?"

"Marnie."

He'd never known a Marnie, but it suited her. "I'm Zach Renfro."

She raised her eyebrows. "Of Renfro Restoration?"

"Have you heard of us?"

She nodded to something behind him. "It's the sign on your truck."

"Oh." He glanced over his shoulder at the Bronco. "Yeah."

"Are you, like, the owner or something?"

"Yeah."

"Oh. Well, Zach Renfro of Renfro Restoration, can you restore this lock to working order?"

"I'll give it a try, Marnie." Her name sat well on his tongue. He wondered how the rest of her would sit.

Zach forced himself to turn his attention to the lock, but even then, he was aware of Marnie's exact location so that when he knelt and her skirt whipped across his upper thigh he felt a warm tingling.

Man, he'd never had it this bad. There was no reason for it. He knew nothing about her. She could be a thief using him to break in.

And he just flat-out didn't care. An old-fashioned word came to mind—smitten. He was smitten by her. She had smit him—could the word be used that way?

Concentrate. "Have you been slamming this door?"

"The wind blew it shut a little while ago."

Zach stood. "The frame has come loose and the lock mechanism is bent a bit, making things stick together pretty good."

"So what does that mean?"

"That means I'm going to have to take the door off the hinges."

"Will that damage it?"

He glanced over his shoulder at her. "Before I got here, you were going to smash the door in."

She gave him a chagrined look. "I forgot about that."

He smiled. She smiled back.

Whoa.

It was like getting hit with a jolt of electricity.

Zach forced himself to turn back to the door hinges. He was so distracted that he grabbed the wrong size screwdriver from his tool belt. "Would you hold this a sec?" he asked, just so he would have an excuse to interact with her.

How pitiful was that?

Not nearly as pitiful as him taking his time while she stood there freezing.

Okay, get a grip. Moments later, Zach set the door aside and Marnie ran into the room. The bedroom, Zach saw, and looked around curiously. There was nothing personal in it. Nice furniture, but nothing to tell him anything about her. It was like a hotel room.

"I am so cold!" She raced over to the bed and reached for a pair of socks that were in two little balls on the floor by a pair of ugly brown hiking shoes.

Zach stood there and watched as Marnie, wearing his jacket and a skirt that outlined her legs, pulled on the socks over unnaturally white feet.

It was the sexiest thing he'd ever seen.

When she finished tugging on her socks, she wiggled her toes. "I just may get the feeling back."

"Here, let me." Zach advanced into the bedroom and knelt at her feet.

Marnie tucked her hair behind both ears. "Uh..."

"Relax." He picked up one sock-clad foot and began quickly rubbing it between both hands, then switched to the other. "How's that?"

"It tingles."

"Tingles are good." He smiled up at her and switched to a slow, deep kneading concentrating on her toes and the ball of her foot. And maybe her leg and the sexy curve of her calf and how the skirt kept climbing northward...

Marnie made a tiny sound, a tiny, devastatingly sexy moan.

Zach looked up. Her face was surrounded by the hair that had slithered out from behind her ears and there was a dazed look in her eyes.

"Feel good?" he asked.

"Oh, yeah. You could do this for a living."

He could do this forever.

Except he was making her nervous, he could tell. She held her arms propped stiffly at her sides and although she let him massage her feet, he guessed she wasn't sure she should. And why should she? They were alone in her bedroom and for all she knew, he could be a carpenter with a foot fetish, if not worse. If he hadn't been so blindsided by...by her, he would have picked up on her feelings sooner. He was just going to have to figure out a way for her to get to know him. Because he sure wanted to know her.

"Does the door lock on you like that very often?" he asked.

"I don't know. This is my first night here."

Zach shifted to the other foot and felt Marnie relax marginally. Encouraged, he continued to talk. "No wonder I haven't seen you around."

And just like that, she stiffened up again. "I—you—actually I walk past here to get to the bus every day."

And he'd missed her? "Did my guys whistle at you?" Is that why she'd withdrawn? "I've been on to them about that. You'd think it was the fifties or something."

"No." Her voice sounded flat. "They didn't whistle at me." She shifted. "I think my feet are okay now. Thanks."

"No problem." Zach could feel her closing him out. He'd been making progress, too. Standing, his gaze fell on the door, which he'd propped against the opening. "Let me take a look at that lock, as long as I'm here."

"You don't have to do that," she said quickly. "I'll let the landlord know and he can have it fixed."

She was giving him the brush-off. If he'd been in his right mind, Zach would have backed off.

But clearly, he wasn't in his right mind. "It would be tomorrow at the earliest before someone could get here and in the meantime, you'd freeze." As he spoke, he walked over to the door and began unscrewing the lock. It was a button-spring type and a little tightening would keep it from falling into the locked position if the door should slam again.

"Are you sure you know what you're doing?" she asked.

Loaded question. "I've installed a lock or two in my time."

"Oh. Duh. Of course you have."

Because he was trying to stall and figure out a way to regain the ground he'd inexplicably lost with her, the lock was an easy fix. In ten seconds it was back to normal. Now, if he'd wanted to get out of here, it would have taken forever.

"All done," he said. "I'll reattach the door and you're good to go."

"Thank you. I really appreciate you helping me."

This was his opportunity to ask her out, but he couldn't come up with anything that didn't sound like a cheesy come-on or make her feel obligated to accept or worse, scare her off.

"I really owe you," she said. "Would you let me buy you a cup of coffee? Or a sandwich if you haven't eaten?"

Yes! Zach nearly gouged the doorjamb with his

screwdriver. Calm down. "Coffee sounds great. I need to put away the ladder and lock up across the street. I'll be five minutes, tops."

Marnie reached for the hiking boots and started lacing them up. "Okay."

He was going to get to spend some more time with her and it made him so darn happy, he couldn't stop grinning. Zach finished reattaching the door, then opened and closed it, testing the lock until he was satisfied.

He hooked a thumb over his shoulder. "I'll just go out the way I came."

"I'll meet you downstairs—hey. Here's your jacket."

She held it out to him and he slipped his arms into it, smelling a sweet scent that he thought was shampoo or lotion or soap rather than perfume. Whatever, feeling the warmth from her body and the sweet scent on his jacket made him irrationally happy and a little turned on. He didn't know what had come over him and he didn't really care. He was just going to go with it.

He stopped for one last look at her before climbing down the ladder. She was shrugging into a navy-blue parka with hot-pink, yellow and lime-green zigzags.

Zach blinked, then blinked again. He'd swear he'd seen that ski jacket before. Where? He frowned as he concentrated and then he remembered—the blob—the runaway the other night had worn a jacket just like that one. And this morning he'd seen Franco open the door to her. Which meant...what did it mean?

THE CONSTRUCTION GUY was named Zach Renfro.

Zach Renfro had golden-brown hair and golden-brown eyes and golden-brown skin and the whitest smile she'd ever seen. Zach Renfro was a hunk, a complete and total hunk by anyone's definition. Complete and total hunks did not often intersect Marnie's life orbit, and not only was this complete and total hunk in her bedroom, he'd just given her the best foot rub of her life.

Okay, so it was the *only* foot rub she'd ever had from a hunk or anyone else, but foot rubs couldn't get better than that.

Life could sure turn on a dime.

Yes, the being in her bedroom part was because he was fixing her door and it really didn't count. She knew that. But just try convincing her racing heart.

As for the hunk part, well, she'd known he was a hunk before, but now she really knew, just as she really knew that such a man did not have women pals, which was apparently Marnie's specialty. The women in his life were lovers, potential lovers or former lovers and lots of them. Besides, who'd want the torture of being his pal?

Not Marnie.

She'd studied his hands as they'd massaged her feet and noticed the tiny scars of various ages and shapes as well as the short fingernails that proclaimed that he worked with his hands.

She worked with her hands, too, but typing wasn't the same.

He'd rescued her. Not that she couldn't have rescued herself, but he hadn't had to resort to breaking glass.

And, wonder of wonders, he didn't recognize her as the idiot who'd shouted lewd remarks at him from the sidewalk.

It was a second chance.

Yeah, but to do what?

Somebody who was girlfriend material would know, said a little voice.

I thought you were supposed to be on my side, she grumbled back at it.

I am. Abandon hope.

But Marnie wasn't going to abandon anything. In a couple of minutes Zach was going to finish the door and leave, so she screwed up her courage and invited him for coffee.

Wonder of wonders, he accepted.

She hoped Franco wouldn't mind if she wore the skirt and quickly grabbed her jacket before Zach noticed that she was wearing her T-shirt inside out.

She debated pulling her hair back into its customary ponytail, but decided to leave it alone since things were going so well.

And then she turned around and saw that things were not going well.

Frowning, Zach stared at her and Marnie realized what had happened: he recognized her, or more likely, her jacket.

One look at his face told her she was Marnie, the antigirlfriend once again.

Well, that little fantasy hadn't lasted very long.

"Yeah, it's me," she said and removed her jacket. She wouldn't be going anywhere now.

"You're the runaway?" His voice sounded thin.

"I'm not a runaway," she began, then stopped. Hadn't she rented this place partly to get away from the status quo? She laughed. "I guess I am a runaway."

"What are you running from?" Amazingly he was still there.

"Me." Marnie sank onto the bed. "But I keep finding myself."

A corner of his mouth tilted up. "Most people want to find themselves."

"And then what? What are you supposed to do with yourself?"

"Live your life, I guess."

"What if you don't like your life?"

He stared at her for a long time—long enough to prompt her to ask, "What?"

"Why were you on the balcony, Marnie?" He spoke in one of those carefully calm voices people use when they don't want to set off another person.

"The fern blew over and I was setting it back up. Why?"

He said nothing, so Marnie thought back over their conversation until she figured it out.

"No, I was not going to jump. And I am not going to jump, nor do I have any inclination to jump. Sheesh."

"Good, 'cause you owe me a cup of coffee."

It was her turn to stare at him. "You still want to go?"

"You bet. If I remember correctly, you said I had a cute butt."

Groaning, Marnie covered her face with her hands. "I'd hoped you'd forgotten about that."

"Why? It made my day."

Marnie gave him a chagrined look. "How pathetic."

He flashed those white teeth at her. "Get your coat on. Downstairs in five." He closed the French doors behind him and disappeared over the side of the balcony.

Marnie didn't know what was worse—Zach being nice, which made her seem even more pitiful, or Zach saying adios and pointedly ignoring her every day when she walked past.

Marnie trudged down the stairs and found Franco standing at the bottom with his arms full of mail and packages while he talked to a young teenage girl, who wore the popular uniform of draggy jeans and a midriff-baring top. It looked like a serious conversation and they both broke off abruptly when they became aware of Marnie on the stairs.

"Ah, Marnie. Do you mind if we take Darcy here on our outing? She lives in one of the apartments."

How could Marnie have forgotten that she was supposed to go to the neighborhood grocery store with Franco?

Zach Renfro, that's how.

"Actually, I need a rain check. While you were gone, I got locked out on the balcony and Zach, the construction guy from across the street, rescued me and fixed the lock."

Franco's face lit up. "He did?"

"You knew the lock was broken?"

"Of course not. I'm talking about him rescuing you. This sounds very exciting. Tell all."

"There's not much to tell. He got a ladder and climbed up. I've offered to buy him a cup of coffee as a thank-you. It's the least I could do."

"The very least." Franco gave her a slight frown.

Marnie rolled her eyes. "I'll get him a sandwich, too, if he wants one."

Franco winced. "A little graciousness would not be amiss." Franco looked at the girl next to him. "You pay attention, too."

Darcy shrugged in the bored way of all teenagers.

"I'll be polite," Marnie protested.

"Aim for enchanting. Perhaps you'll hit pleasant."

Marnie thought of Zach's expression when he recognized her and felt her spirits sink even lower. "What's the point?"

"Practice. That's the point."

Zach as practice material... "It's a good point."

"I want you to remember everything and be prepared to tell me in complete detail."

"Why?" Marnie asked.

"Because I want to know."

"Just tell him. It's easier," offered Darcy. "He'll bug you until you do, anyway."

"Oh, Franco, not for the script. I doubt it's going to be very excit—"

Franco gasped. "What are you wearing?"

Marnie looked down at herself. "The skirt—I didn't think you'd mind."

"I'm talking about the horror of your shoes."

They all looked at Marnie's feet. "These are the only ones I brought. I like them. I can walk in them."

"Not even the skirt can overcome those shoes," he was mumbling as Zach opened the door to the foyer.

"Think of it as an eclectic look." Marnie left before Franco could start questioning Zach.

"Eclectic, ecshmelectic," she heard him mutter behind her and smiled. Franco was something else.

"Where are we going?" Zach asked after they'd walked in silence for half a block because Marnie couldn't think of anything to say.

"There's a coffee place just down the street. I pass it on the way to the bus, but I've never stopped there. I usually go to the Starbucks next to where I work."

"And where is that?" he asked politely.

"Carnahan Custom Software. I write code."

She sensed him studying her. He did that a lot. "What?" she asked.

"You don't look like a computer geek."

"Yes, I do. I look exactly like a computer geek." She stopped walking and stuck out a foot to show him her hiking boots. "I revel in my geekiness."

Zach laughed. Marnie liked making him laugh and just like that, she got an idea.

He could give her tips on the whole dating thing. Realistically, he wasn't going to stick around for her to practice on after tonight unless she worked out some kind of deal with him.

And by the time they reached the Caffeine Connection, she knew exactly what she could offer.

AS THEY WALKED, Marnie dropped little tidbits about herself, just superficial stuff, but Zach gathered them up and squirreled them away.

He was mesmerized by her. Everything she said seemed profound and everything she did fascinated him. He thought her boots were quirky and her skirt was sexy and her parka was...big. But the way she burrowed her chin in it to ward off the cold looked cute. Her hair blew all around and the tips of her ears were pink. Zach liked long hair. The pink ears he could take or leave.

The rational part of Zach knew that no woman was the *uber* woman he'd made Marnie out to be, but the irrational part was in control. And the irrational part wanted to spend as much time as possible with her. The irrational part wanted to get his hands on her.

The irrational part might get him arrested.

He recalled in vivid detail the feel of her feet and calves. If that skin was soft and smooth, then how smooth would the skin that never saw the light of day feel? He felt the same curiosity and anticipation as he did when peeling back the layers on the walls of one of his Painted Ladies to discover the hidden treasures underneath.

Zach inhaled deeply and shut down those thoughts pronto. He had a long way to go before he'd be peeling off any layers from Marnie.

They ordered coffee and split a giant roasted chicken breast with honey mustard sandwich.

Zach didn't like honey-mustard sauce. Either the honey or the mustard, but don't mix them. And yet he happily ate the sandwich because Marnie liked it.

He was turning into a complete wuss.

Incredibly, it got worse.

"You know, that day...the other day," she began.

Zach wanted to forget that day—not all of it, just the part where he'd mistaken her for a homeless person.

"Your crew whistled at these two women."

Damn. "I apologize—"

"No, no. The thing is, they didn't whistle at me."

Uh-oh. What could he say?

"And it was right after I'd been out with some guys from work."

"Your boyfriend?" She'd better not have a boyfriend.

She made a noise. "Hardly. In fact they let me know that I definitely wasn't the girlfriend type." And then she proceeded to tell him about some jerk named Barry, and it was clear that she was hung up on him.

"So I was wondering if you would do me a favor," Marnie asked.

"Shove Barry's teeth down his throat?" That's one favor Zach could get into.

"Teach me how to become girlfriend material."

"Huh?" he said eloquently.

"I don't do it right, so I need some pointers."

While Zach grappled with figuring out exactly what "it" she meant, Marnie went on.

"Look, I know I'm not your type."

Admittedly, she wasn't his usual type. But his usual type had never worked out. Maybe she was his new type. "How do you know that?"

"Please. It's okay. Not everybody is everybody's

type. But I need a few lessons before I can be anybody's type." She was serious.

"To get this Barry?" No effing way.

"No!" she said with reassuring force. "I just want him to change his mind about me, but I'm going to need help."

"Yeah, yeah. You want him to want you so you can get revenge by rejecting him." Zach shook his head. "That never works because deep down, you really do want him, so when you get to the rejection part, you can't go through with it."

Marnie perked up. "Ooo. This sounds like experience talking."

"What can I say? I was young once. I'm telling you, forget this Barry and move on." He gave her his best I'm-interested-and-available smile.

She was oblivious. Women were not often oblivious to Zach, and he didn't know what to make of it.

"I can't move on! Don't you understand? He and the guys completely dismissed me as woman."

"Ignore them. They are idiots."

"I know. The point is for them to *know* they are idiots. But I need girlfriend practice. Or maybe it should be boyfriend practice. Either way, even Franco said so."

Frank needed to mind his own business. "So find a boyfriend. Then by definition, you become a girlfriend."

"If I could do that, then this whole conversation would be irrelevant."

Either she'd come up with a novel and effective approach to interest men—particularly him—or she needed as much help as she thought because Zach was doing his best to convince her that the conversation *was* irrelevant. He leaned forward and lowered his voice. "You're sure you're not my type?"

There was a flash in her eyes, kind of a deer-in-the-headlights look and he thought he'd gotten through to her. But then she clamped her lips together and looked away. "Please stop being so nice."

Now that wasn't something a guy heard all the time.

The fog that had enveloped him ever since he'd first set eyes on her cleared a little and he realized that her self-esteem had taken a beating by her jerk of a coworker.

Zach, himself, hadn't helped either. He looked at her, really studied her. While she was incredibly appealing to him at this moment, he could step back and acknowledge that others might not see the same appeal.

They would see that she wore no makeup. Her hair was long, but not styled. And her clothes were unique. Now that he'd been around her, Zach considered them part of the way she was, but that coat she wore was so big it was like a turtle's shell. Her shoes got the job done, but they weren't the sexy little things he'd seen other women wear. She was completely without artifice both in manner and appearance. Marnie was the real thing. It might be a sign he was getting older, but Zach found he appreciated the real thing.

Zach had always been able to see potential. Maybe that's what drew him to Marnie. She was like one of his houses before he got to it—plain, without the color and gingerbread trim. With a little trim, a little attitude...

"I wouldn't expect you to do this for nothing," she was saying. "In return, I'd build you a killer Web site."

Zach still wasn't sure this was a good idea. "I have a Web site. A professional designed it."

"But I didn't design it." She smiled slightly. "And I'm the best."

Zach actually stopped breathing. If only he had a camera to capture Marnie's expression as she sat across the table and the incredible way her mouth tilted against the coffee mug. Supreme self-confidence was supremely sexy.

"My guy said he was the best." Zach wanted to tweak her a little. "And he charged like it, too."

Shaking her head, she sipped her coffee. "You couldn't afford the site I'd design for you. I'm talking flash, sound, movies—all the razzle-dazzle. All custom. Already I have an idea for the opening page—a big, shabby *R* appears and gets renovated. The site'll look great, especially since there won't be budget constraints." She grinned.

As she talked, Zach felt a connection between them. She could have been quoting him: *"You can't afford it, but I'm doing it anyway just out of pride. Just because I can. because I want to."*

Zach understood that. He lived that. And to find a woman who felt the same way...

"Okay, deal," he heard himself say. Not because he cared about a flashy Web site, but because this was apparently the only way he'd get to be with her. And he had to be with her.

She may not know it, but she was still hung up on this Barry guy and she would be until the jerk acknowledged her as a desirable woman.

Zach could save them all a lot of time and prove that she was a desirable woman right here and now, but Marnie wouldn't believe him, thanks to those morons she worked with.

So Zach was going to give her all the dating lessons she wanted. But he had no intention of handing her over to Barry. Barry had missed out. End of story.

4

THE SKIRT'S POWER is tremendous and is not affected by distance. Within moments of M. putting on the skirt, she attracted a construction worker from across the street. From his dazed and all but drooling expression, I have concluded that he was definitely under the influence of the skirt.

M. is what we in the biz call a "diamond in the rough." Fortunately, she is aware that she needs polishing and has promised to go shopping today. I have booked a style and makeup lesson with Cecily at the New Dawn Hair Salon and Boutique. (Note to self: investigate as possible set for scene.) Naturally, I could do M.'s makeup, but I am more prone to the dramatic stage makeup which is not needed here.

I must note that the skirt demonstrates its remarkable power under the most difficult of circumstances. I am stunned. Utterly stunned.

Tonight, M. will practice her wiles on the construction worker, whom I shall investigate for suitability.

"YOU SHOULD HAVE asked me before you made an appointment, Franco! I might have had to work through lunch!" From her seat at the stylist's station, Marnie scowled at the platinum blonde with spiky hair. If Cecily and Franco thought they were chopping off all her hair like that...well, she wouldn't let them.

They ignored her. Cecily kept picking up hanks of her hair and dropping them. "Layers."

Franco nodded. "I'll leave her in your hands while I pop into the back and see what I find."

"I just got some cute tops in." Cecily began brushing Marnie's hair.

Franco took Marnie's color swatches and headed toward the salon's boutique.

I must be crazy to do this, Marnie thought. But she was going to see Zach tonight for her first lesson and then she wouldn't be back in the apartment until next week. So she might as well submit to this now.

Cecily held up a length of Marnie's hair. "I need to take off an inch to an inch and a half to get rid of the dead ends."

Marnie nodded and refrained from pointing out that all hair was dead.

"Let's get the conditioner on you, then."

"I only have an hour for lunch...." Nobody was listening to her. It was a good thing she had about a thousand hours of unpaid overtime to her credit.

Marnie was lying on her back with her head hanging in the sink and her hair soaking up conditioner faster than a desert in a rainstorm when Franco appeared above her.

"Look what I found." A bright turquoise sweater appeared in her line of vision. "Your color. It comes in red, too."

Marnie liked the color, but it was a thin short-sleeved knit. "I'll get cold in that."

"I knew you'd say that." Franco held up the other arm. "Matching long-sleeved sweater. What do you think?"

"It's awfully small."

"It stretches in all the right places."

Marnie clutched her bulky cable-knit sweater to her. "Does it come in a large?"

"Yes, but I'm not selling it to you," Cecily said. "In fact you might need a petite."

"What?"

"Hmm." Franco shook his head. "There's a fine line between sexy and slutty."

"How would you know?" Cecily grinned and started rinsing Marnie's hair.

Franco sniffed. "Hon, you haven't seen that line in years. Marnie, I want you to buy the tomato-red, too."

Marnie opened her eyes and saw a flash of red before the water spray made her close them again. "Fine. Whatever."

"Fabulous. I'll put these by the front. And now, I must be off. Marnie, next week we'll tackle slacks. For tonight, you can borrow the black skirt and wear one of the tops. Cecily will do your makeup. Cecily, she's Deep Autumn."

"Makeup?" Marnie looked warily at Cecily's heavy black eyeliner.

"I don't need a chart to know what'll look good on her." Cecily wrapped a towel around Marnie's head.

Marnie spoke up, "Makeup isn't really my thing."

"She needs the chart," Franco said.

"I'm not sure about the makeup."

"Hush, Marnie." Franco inhaled sharply. "I forgot

about the shoes." He looked at his watch. "What size are you?"

"Seven-and-a-half B."

"You need to start carrying shoes, Cecily."

"Too much trouble. You can come on back," she said to Marnie.

"I'll see what I can do." Franco left the sweaters hanging on a rack by the front door. The bell clanged as he hurried out.

"You know, you ought to let me put highlights in here sometime." Cecily dragged a wide-toothed comb through Marnie's wet hair.

"This is enough change for one day," Marnie said.

"Yeah. Anyways you'd have to book a couple of hours." Cecily sectioned off Marnie's hair and picked up a pair of scissors.

To distract herself, Marnie asked, "How did you meet Franco?"

"He comes in here for his manicures."

Marnie had never heard of a man getting a manicure. Cecily picked up her hand. "You could use one. You got a big date tonight?"

"It's not exactly a date. It's more of a tutoring session."

"You mean like for math or something?"

"Something," Marnie said because Cecily was definitely not the type to understand someone needing girlfriend lessons.

Marnie was just getting used to not flinching every time Cecily held her hair straight above her head and took off chunks when Franco came bustling in carrying two shoe boxes. "One of these has to work because I am *so* late."

"Those had better be flats," Marnie warned.

Franco said nothing as he attempted to unlace, then pry off, Marnie's hiking books. Marnie finally had to take them off herself.

Franco opened the first box and showed her a black backless shoe. "Mules with kitten heels."

"Cute," Cecily pronounced.

"Oh, come on." Marnie took the shoe. "How am I supposed to keep this on my foot and actually walk in it?"

"You can walk in it, but you won't go hiking in it. Put it on," Franco directed.

Marnie hopped out of the chair, ignoring the mound of clippings all around. Did she have any hair left on her head? "This shoe has to have been designed by some man to oppress women by keeping them helpless." She pulled up the leg of her jeans and slipped her foot into the shoe. "Why on earth would any woman wear..." She looked down at her foot. "Can I put on the other one?"

Silently, Franco handed her the other shoe.

"Have you got a mirror?"

Cecily pointed toward the boutique. Marnie, wet hair and all, walked gingerly toward the full-length mirror. It was easier once she stepped onto the carpet. After pacing back and forth in front of the mirror and staring at her feet the entire time, she got the hang of walking in the shoes.

They were darling and cute and precious and all

those other words she'd never had a reason to use before.

She was still staring in the mirror when Franco joined her. "I have pretty feet," she said. "What's in the other box?"

"Mules, thicker heel, black and white woven leather with silver accents. A springier look, I thought."

Marnie held out her hand. "Give them to me."

Franco handed them over and Marnie eagerly put them on.

"Oh." She kept staring at her feet and how they looked in the shoes. "They're beautiful. Can I have both pairs?"

A knowing smile creased Franco's face. "That's between you and your charge card, my dear."

Zombielike, Marnie walked—more proficiently this time—back to the waiting Cecily, got her charge card out of her purse and gave the card to Franco.

"I'll have the clerk bring the receipt for you to sign," he said. "I must go. I'll see you tonight."

"Thanks, Franco."

"My pleasure." He air-kissed both her and Cecily. "Cecily, talk her into a pedicure."

"You got time?" Cecily asked.

Marnie stared at her feet in the black-and-white shoes. "Can I have red toenails?"

"Sure."

"I've got time."

ALL DAY LONG, Marnie had been in Zach's thoughts. He would see her tonight for dinner and he had absolutely no idea how to begin her "lessons."

He'd always thought this sort of thing was instinctive. It was for him. And his instincts had been working overtime.

Zach climbed down the ladder where he'd been measuring some damaged crown molding in the front parlor. He was going to keep as much of the original as possible but it was a royal pain to match the pattern and make it look seamless. Still, that was the difference between restoring and remodeling.

He was penciling cut marks on a piece of wood when Franco stuck his head into the room. "A moment of your time, please."

Great. Zach didn't have time to fraternize with the neighbors, especially when he wanted to get this finished in time to shower and change before picking up Marnie. "I'm kinda busy," he hinted.

"As am I." Ignoring the hint, Franco walked around the ladder. "You are going out with Marnie tonight." It wasn't a question.

"Yes, any objection?" Like it would matter if he had.

"I don't know yet. Give me your social security number."

At that, Zach straightened and tossed his pencil down. "What—are you going to have me investigated?"

Franco met his gaze squarely. "Yes."

"Save your money. I'm not an ax-murderer."

Smiling, Franco said, "I have a friend. She's very efficient, but it's faster with the social security number."

Zach heard an underlying firmness in Franco's voice that surprised him. It was the kind of firmness that meant a man could back up what he said. Interesting. "Just tell me something—what do you care?"

Franco didn't back down. "Marnie is intelligent, but somewhat naive. She met you because she has rented my apartment. Therefore, I consider myself responsible for her well-being."

Zach did not want to like this character, but damn. Here was a man accepting responsibility in a time when a lot of men ran from it. He had to admire the guy for that, even if his weathervane pointed east instead of west.

So Zach gave him the social security number, then wrote his driver's license number on the back of a business card and gave that to Franco, too.

"I'm not going to find anything untoward, am I?" Franco asked.

"Nope. Want my parent's address?"

"Do they live here in San Francisco?"

"Yeah."

"Yes, please."

Zach rattled off his parents' Pacific Heights address, knowing it would impress Franco. Should impress Franco.

Franco wrote it down without comment. "One more thing—Marnie has made a real effort this afternoon. You might compliment her."

Zach gave him a look. "I *have* done this before."

"I'm sure you have." Franco closed his notebook. "This will do. Thank you very much."

Nonplussed, Zach stared after him as he left.

MARNIE STARED at herself in the bedroom mirror as she tried to get used to her new appearance. And, also, because she couldn't choose between the shoes. Or the tops. With such pressure, how did other women get dressed every day?

At last, she settled on the red and the all-black shoes because she had red toenails. She'd never even looked at her feet before, yet now, she couldn't stop staring at them. Her legs seemed different, too. They now looked worthy of the skirt. She couldn't keep borrowing it from Franco, so she'd better buy one like it.

As for the makeup, well, the jury was out on that. She'd submitted to some horrendous torture called an eyebrow wax and her brows still felt tender. In spite of Cecily's punk rock look, she'd applied the cosmetics with a light hand, but Marnie's face still looked different. All the proportions had changed.

In fact, everything looked different. Marnie flipped her hair over her shoulder and watched as it rippled and shone, just like an ad for conditioner on TV.

She'd never even made it back to the office this afternoon because once she got started on the beauty treatments, she couldn't stop. How could she have her toes done and neglect her fingers?

It was called a French manicure, which basically made the pink part pinker and the white part whiter. Marnie wasn't ready for red fingernails…yet.

Then there was the aromatherapy facial and the chair shoulder massage. Add the makeup and the eyebrows and the blow-dry and there went the afternoon. Other women couldn't do this all the time because how else could they go to work and lead normal lives?

Never mind her credit card bill. Amortization was

the key here. She could have been indulging herself at beauty salons for the past ten years and hadn't.

She'd even bought underwear, something Franco hadn't mentioned, thank goodness. Only Marnie wasn't so sure about the underwear. The bra had liquid-filled inserts that made her look Barbie-dollish. She could take them out, but if she was going to do this, then she was going to do it right. But was Barbie doll right or wrong?

Zach would tell her if it was too much.

Marnie put on the matching long-sleeved top, grabbed her jacket and headed down the stairs, carefully putting one foot in front of the other. Her toes were going to cramp from trying to keep the shoes on, but they'd look good while doing so.

Franco was hanging up the lobby telephone when Marnie made it to the bottom of the stairs. "Hey, Franco. What do you think?" She held out her arms and turned around.

"Oh, Marnie." Franco steepled his fingers over a smile. "This is going to be great. May I watch?"

"Watch what? I look okay, don't I?"

"You look better than okay and you know it. Except—" he held out his hand "—the coat stays here."

Marnie clutched the coat to her. "I'll freeze! My legs are bare! My toes are bare!"

"Mr. Renfro will make sure you don't get cold. Marnie—the coat."

The coat was for more than warmth and Marnie suspected Franco knew it. It wasn't that cold outside. It was just that she still had bra issues. Reluctantly, she walked across the foyer and handed him the coat.

Franco tugged it gently from her resisting fingers. "What do you know about Zach Renfro, Marnie?"

"He owns Renfro Restoration and he seems nice."

Franco sighed heavily. "Lucky for you, he is nice." Franco picked up his ever-present notebook. "In fact, two more white-bread people, I have never met. I don't know what you'll find to talk about."

"What is that supposed to mean?" She peered at his notes. "Did you have him investigated?"

"Yes, as you should have done."

Marnie's jaw dropped. "I can't believe you!"

"You're too trusting. You need to be more aware."

"This isn't New York, Franco." She'd learned he'd lived there before.

"No, it's San Francisco." He gave her a look that was stern, even for him.

"But isn't having Zach investigated a little extreme?"

"Expedient." Franco was unrepentant. "And now we know he all but walks on water." For some reason, this seemed to irritate Franco.

"So what did you find out?"

Franco held the notebook next to his chest. "I have to leave you *something* to talk about. But I must say that both of you are frighteningly upstanding citizens."

"What's so frightening about that?" Marnie gave the skirt a swish, liking the feel of it against her legs.

"Because you have the turmoil of rebellion still within you. One day you're both going to snap. I will ask only that you please snap in front of me."

"No one is going to snap."

Franco raised an eyebrow. "And how much did you spend today?"

"A lot." Marnie admired her feet. "It was worth it."

"The thin edge of the wedge," Franco pronounced ominously. "I'm going to position my chair for the grand entry. You should stand to the right of the stairs. Stomach in, chest..." He coughed. "Chest out."

"Why don't I just hike up the skirt and stick out my thumb?"

"Don't even jest. I'm serious. You will cause wrecks."

Marnie grinned and stuck out her foot. "It's the toenails, right?"

Franco snorted.

ZACH HAD TO PARK in front of the underground garage entrance so when he looked through the window and saw Marnie already downstairs talking with Franco, he was relieved. In his experience, traffic tickets were a bad way to begin an evening.

The screen door squeaked as he opened first it and then the front door. "Hey, I like a woman who doesn't keep a man wai—ting."

He stopped and the screen door hit him in the back. After that, everything happened in slow motion, like one of those allergy commercials with people bounding through pollen-laden fields.

Marnie—and it had to be Marnie because Franco was holding her coat—turned around, her shiny hair rippling across her face and flowing down her back in one perfect wave. Her smile lit up her face, a face that had huge brown eyes and pretty pink lips.

Her clothes had shrunk and she'd ditched the clodhoppers.

She was a stunner.

And he was stunned.

"Loving it. I'm just loving it." Franco dropped the coat behind him and started writing in a notebook.

"Hi, Zach," Marnie said softly.

He couldn't speak. She was...she was...she was every high-school boy's prom dream. She was the college crush. She was the one a guy wanted to bring home to meet his parents. She was that elusive perfect mix of prim, proper and provocative. He narrowed his eyes. She was too good to be true.

"Stunned into speechlessness," Franco murmured as he wrote.

The longer he looked, the more suspicious Zach became. "Is this some kind of joke?"

Marnie's smile faltered.

"Or a test? One of those TV shows with the hidden cameras? Are you a twin?"

Franco wrote furiously. "Better than anything I could have made up."

Zach stalked over to him. "What's going on?"

Franco sighed and set aside his notebook. "Marnie is in the process of reaching her full feminine potential."

"I'd say she reached it and vaulted over it."

"Auugh!" Franco grabbed for the notebook. "Just let me write that down...."

"Leave the damn notebook alone and tell me what's going on!"

"What's going on is that you're acting weird." Marnie came over to stand beside Franco.

Franco got to his feet. "No one mentioned such a temper in the report. I'm not sure I should allow Marnie to go out with you."

Zach had had enough of Frank and his reports and notebooks. "Like you could stop me."

"Certainly I could. I have a black belt—"

"Sure you do. Come on, Marnie. I want some answers." Zach reached for her arm.

And found his hand blocked. He hadn't even seen Franco move. He tried again and was just as efficiently blocked again. He gave an experimental push and felt nothing give. The guy was all wiry muscle. The wiry ones always had something to prove.

Marnie clapped her hands. "Franco, that is so cool! I didn't know you could do that!"

"I can do much more, as Mr. Renfro will discover should he persist in his unwanted attentions."

"They're not unwanted," Marnie said.

"Mr. Renfro believes you." Zach dropped his arm. "But Mr. Renfro can fight dirty if he needs to."

"Fling your dirt if you must."

"Back off guys," Marnie said. "Zach, what is your problem?"

What was his problem? "You...look different," he grumbled.

Her smile disappeared. "And you don't like the way I look? 'Cause I do. It's real high-maintenance, so it's not an everyday thing, but it's fun for a change."

Fun for a change. Zach didn't know if he could stand this much change. He closed his eyes briefly. "I like the way you look. I liked the way you looked yesterday, too, but...damn it, Marnie, you should give a guy some warning." His gaze traveled over her, taking in the red sweater and the skirt that carved her legs in a way that tricked him into thinking he saw more than he did.

"Wait a minute...you were mad because I look too good?"

"The light dawns," Franco said. "He thought we were playing a trick on him. I've said it before and I'll say it again, a well-shaped eyebrow is as good as a face-lift."

"Nah." Marnie stuck out her foot. "It's my red toenails, isn't it, Zach?"

He looked down one well-shaped leg to the foot he remembered rubbing and saw the wiggling red-tipped toes she was clearly proud of. There was something about the red toenails against the milky-white skin. They looked strangely intimate.

Intimate thoughts about toes? What had happened to him? When he'd had intimate thoughts about women's body parts in the past, toes had never made the list. Until now. He swallowed. "I need to start over if Mr. Black Belt here has no objection."

"Good idea," Franco murmured.

"Marnie...you look..." Zach spread his hands. "Amazing."

Marnie stood still for a moment, then glanced at Franco. "Is that good?"

"Amazing is good," Franco said. "Run along children."

Zach took Marnie's arm.

She beamed at him. "Franco said you wouldn't let me get cold."

"Remind me not to underestimate that guy." Zach took a deep breath. Being around her made it necessary for him to concentrate on actions he normally shouldn't have to think about. Like breathing. "I need to apologize for back there. But it's tricky. You do look great, but I don't want you to think you didn't look okay before, you know? I guess it's that you look good in a different way."

"So you're saying that I should go for this look when I go out with guys?"

Zach didn't like the thought of her out with other guys.

Bad sign. That meant he was already at the possessive stage and to be honest, he didn't know how he got there.

True, she looked hot tonight, but he'd been drawn to her when she'd been only warm.

"Am I allowed to tell you that you look good, too?" she asked. "'Cause you do."

"You're allowed within reason—and sometimes unreasonably depending on the circumstances—to do whatever you want."

"I meant—is it girlfriend behavior?"

Right. That. "Why do you think you need to be taught this?"

"I explained."

"Yeah, you did, but I'm not buying it. Not when you look like that. How about we go find this Barney or Barry right now? We'll let him drool a little and then he can eat our dust."

Marnie laughed as they reached his car and he opened the door for her. "You're so funny."

Zach hadn't been kidding.

Marnie stepped in the car, hesitated then stepped back out. "Not used to heels and a skirt," she muttered. "Sit and swivel." She grinned up at Zach. "I'm channeling my mother's voice. It's amazing how that stuff can be buried for years and then pops up when you need it."

She proceeded to get into the car in a fluid movement of legs and skirt with a flash of red toes.

Zach stood there staring down at the skirt, the legs...and the red toes. Nothing he hadn't seen before. Nothing that should make him act irrationally.

Nothing that should make him want to get into the car and drive and drive until he and Marnie ended up totally alone with no chance of encountering another human being.

He closed the door with quiet deliberation and inhaled deeply of the exhaust fumes emanating from the garage, hoping to clear his head because his head must need clearing.

She was just a woman. A little on the quirky side and quirky normally didn't do it for him. That would be normally because this situation wasn't normal.

So that was his goal for the evening—normalization. Zach opened the car door. He'd break this inexplicable attraction or at least control it instead of letting it control him. He inhaled another lungful of exhaust. Control. He was in control.

5

ZACH GOT INTO the car and glanced over at Marnie, who was having trouble adjusting the shoulder belt between her breasts, stretching the sweater ever tighter.

His fingers spasmed on the steering wheel and he stared straight ahead, focusing all his attention on the traffic light. He was so not in control.

A car horn blasted.

"You're blocking the entrance to the garage," Marnie offered.

Zach put his car into gear and shot down the street with tires squealing. The light was yellow and at the last minute, he decided not to go through the intersection and had to brake hard.

"You haven't put on your seat belt, and if you're going to drive like that, you really should."

Zach jammed the shoulder belt into position. "Okay, lesson number one. Do not, under any circumstances, criticize a man's driving."

"Even if it's bad?"

"You wouldn't be criticizing it if it were good, would you?"

"Got it. No comments on driving. Am I allowed to ask if I can drive?"

"No. The guy drives. Always."

"What if it's my car?"

"Do you have a car?"

"No."

"Then it's not an issue."

"What if I buy a car?"

"The guy drives."

At some point the light changed. Zach only realized it when the driver behind him honked. Irritated, he ground the gears, which irritated him further, and lurched into the intersection, then sped down the hill.

"What if the guy drives like a bat out of hell?" Marnie asked.

"Don't date him."

"Well, I won't know how he drives ahead of time, will I?"

A stale green light shone at the next intersection. Zach hesitated and then slowed, thinking it would turn yellow at any moment. Did it? No. So he braked and crept to an intersection lit by the glow of a yellow light. He was completely stopped before it changed to red, earning him another honk from the driver behind and a series of gestures that he saw in the rearview mirror.

He'd not only lost control of his libido, he'd lost control of his driving.

"I'm glad this isn't a real date," Marnie said into the silence. "Because I'm thinking that you need to find a balance in your driving and I couldn't say that if this were a real date, could I?"

She sure talked a lot. "No."

The light turned green and, predictably, the driver

behind him honked. Zach resisted the urge to accelerate slowly in retaliation.

"Am I allowed to ask where we're going?"

"You should know where you're going in advance," he snapped.

"You haven't told me where we're going," she pointed out.

"You didn't ask."

"You told me not to!"

"Actually, what I said was that by the time you're in the car, you should know where you're going."

A beat of silence went by. "Stop the car."

"Marnie..."

"I want to do this right. I'm thinking you've got a good point. Pin down the details ahead of time and it seems like more of a date instead of somebody feeding somebody who has spent hours of her time on a stupid project she won't even get credit for. Or trying to buy her off with beer," she added darkly.

Zach smiled and then he laughed.

"That's better. You've been acting very cranky. I was going to mention that next."

Loss of control did that to a man. "I'm not cranky I'm—" sexually frustrated "—on edge."

"Why?"

She wasn't being coy, she truly didn't know. Zach knew. Zach knew he was the victim of a sudden and strong attraction that he couldn't explain and didn't even want to. He wanted Marnie to be suddenly and strongly attracted to him, too, but either she wasn't, which bruised his pride, or she was and could hide it very, very well.

Certainly better than he was.

He felt as though he'd had a lot of strong coffee without any food and Marnie was a piece of warm apple pie.

Make that hot apple pie.

He inhaled, imagining cinnamon. "It's work stuff."

"Are you gonna tell me about it?"

Why not? "The owners of the Victorian I'm working on have been grumbling about how long the renovation is taking." This was the truth and it would have bothered him more if he hadn't had Marnie on his mind. "But I gave them an estimate up front and I'm right on schedule. They keep reminding me how much it's costing, but here again, they agreed to everything." Of course, he had pushed the scope of the project the way he always did. Zach always used the best of everything, but since he kept labor charges low, people got a real bargain. "I don't take on remodels. I restore."

"What's the difference?"

"I put the building back to its original condition—or the condition it was when it had the most historical significance. Say if somebody famous had lived in that house, I would restore it to the time he lived there, even if the house was, say, fifty years old then."

"You mean if a seventies rock star lived there you'd put lime-green shag carpet back on the floor?"

"*I* wouldn't."

"Oh, so you're not a purist."

"I am!"

"Then you'd have to put the same carpet back on the floor, right?"

"I—" Zach glanced at her to find her grinning at him. "Are you making fun of me?"

"No, I swear! Well, kinda. I wanted to see if you had a sense of humor. Because, you were getting *really* grumpy."

"Situations like this make me grumpy." He told her a little more about the house and the waffling owners. Zach never unloaded on people and surprised himself by telling Marnie so much. He was even more surprised to find that telling her lessened the pressure.

"So, I assume you have a contract—what can the owners do?" she asked.

"Pay costs incurred to date plus the cancellation penalty and the house gets left as is."

Marnie made a dismayed sound. "You mean with all the siding off and everything?"

"Yeah." He sensed her studying him, but he knew better than to risk glancing at her again. He'd just gotten his driving back under control. "So I've been pushing everybody pretty hard to get as much done as possible. Maybe the owners will change their minds."

"The loss of the job isn't what's bothering you—it's leaving the house in that condition. Because even if the owners hire somebody else to finish it—"

"They won't," he said flatly. "Nobody else would touch the job for what I quoted."

"So it'll either be slapped back together or it'll be abandoned and fall apart and you can't stand that, can you?"

No, he couldn't. And Marnie got it. Zach took a deep breath, relaxing for the first time this evening. Uncanny. They hadn't spent much more than an hour together and she was one of the few, outside his family, who understood what drove him. "These are the Victorians that survived the 1906 earthquake and fires. Once they're gone, they're gone. They deserve better."

"Can't your company buy it as a spec house?" she asked. "You can fix it up and sell it for a profit."

Zach shook his head. "I can't spare the capital now." Someday, he'd be more commercial, but he wasn't ready yet.

They spent the next few minutes driving in a comfortable silence. Zach had been thinking about the house and not about Marnie for once which must mean he was returning to normal.

He was congratulating himself when she spoke and set him off again.

"Zach?"

"Yeah?"

"You still didn't tell me where we're going."

"We're going to Seasonings. It's a painfully trendy restaurant and watering hole in SoMa—South of Market—"

"I know what that is."

Of course she did. "We're going there so you can see the singles of San Francisco in action." He faked a very bad British accent. "You can observe their behavior and become familiar with the species."

Marnie laughed.

Zach's voice returned to normal. "And also, because you might be taken there on a date sometime."

"That's very clever of you."

"I do try."

"Have you been there before?"

"I've been to places like it. This one's too new."

"So...you aren't dating anybody?"

How had she figured that out? "No."

"Why not? Or can't I ask?"

"You can ask me, but on a regular date, save the past relationship revelations for later in the evening. Or even better, the second date."

"Okay." Several beats went by. "So—why aren't you dating anybody?" she prompted.

Zach had been prepared for the follow-up question but still struggled to explain. "I was. She...pushed too hard."

"For a commitment?"

"For me to change. She didn't want to accept that I like the way I live and work. It's low-key, low-maintenance and low-income. I did the office bit. Never again."

"So did she ask you to change?"

Zach shifted in his seat. "Not in so many words. But to be fair, we were engaged before I left the office and started restoring the Painted Ladies. I had to liquidate to get enough capital to start the business. Caitlin wasn't too thrilled with my new apartment and the long hours. And she really hated my Bronco. We always had to take her car."

Marnie ran her hands over the leather seats of Zach's Audi TT. "She didn't like this car?"

"I didn't have this car then. I bought it from my dad when he got a new one. Look, our parents are friends and she thought we would live their kind of life."

"Hmm."

Out of the corner of his eye, Zach saw Marnie's fingers playing with the material of her skirt, pleating it and releasing the material. As she did so, it fell softly around her legs. Zach drew in a deep breath. That was some skirt. He couldn't remember ever noticing so much about what a woman wore before, but he noticed everything about Marnie.

Marnie's face was turned away from him as she gazed out the window. "You know," she said, "I'm trying very hard to work up sympathy for you, but you changed your whole lifestyle after she signed on."

Zach gritted his teeth. "I realize that. But I had hoped for more support from my future wife."

"Did you talk about it with her beforehand?"

"She knew restoration is my passion."

"I'm going to take that as a no. Wow."

He should have kept his mouth shut about Caitlin. "I didn't want to be talked out of it."

"Could you have been talked out of it?"

"No."

"But still—it was her life, too."

"Please. I heard all about that. She never gave me a chance. She broke off the engagement within two weeks."

"Well, yeah. She realized there was no future."

"At least not the one she wanted right off the bat. She could have shown a little more faith." He exhaled heavily. "Everyone seems to think this is a phase." That had pretty much been the gist of the lecture he'd received at the end—from Caitlin and his disappointed mother. And Caitlin's mother barely spoke to him now.

Women. He shot a disgusted look at Marnie, which she missed because she was still looking out the window. He'd thought she was different. He'd thought Marnie would understand because she understood how he felt about the Victorian houses. But for somebody who talked too much, she wasn't saying anything.

He couldn't stand it. "You think I'm wrong, too?"

"About not discussing major life changes with your fianceé—absolutely. About following your dream? Not at all."

Okay, so she did understand. "At least any woman I meet now will know up front that restoring the old Victorians is the most important thing in my life." They were at a stoplight so he could look at her as he spoke.

"The most important?" Marnie laughed. "You haven't met the right woman yet."

SO ZACH WAS ON a noble crusade. Nothing and nobody would divert him from his quest to save the Victorians.

Okay. Message received already. Like she ever thought she had a chance with him, anyway. He was probably cranky because he had to take time from his precious house to give her dating pointers.

At least he'd get a fab Web site out of the deal. By the time she was finished, he'd be *the* restoration specialist in San Francisco. He'd have his pick of projects. Enough to keep him company in his old age because it was obvious that a mere woman wouldn't be enough.

Marnie slid a glance over at him as they approached

the restaurant. Not even a woman who needed her dating skills restored. Yeah, to him, she was probably an amusing side project. Fix up Marnie and send her on her way.

Pity.

She could hear the music from Seasonings as the parking attendant opened her door. By the time she figured out the reverse of sit and swivel, Zach was standing outside the car door, extending his hand.

After the valet drove off, she paused and looked around her. "The city is so beautiful at night. And I can enjoy being here knowing I won't have to end the evening with an hour commute to get home."

"Why don't you move into town? Too expensive?" Zach put his hand in the small of her back to guide her toward the entrance.

It was unconscious possessiveness and Marnie liked the way it felt. For a change. "That and I wanted to be there for my mom after my dad died. I do pay her rent, but it's nothing like I'd have to pay to live in my own apartment here." She laughed. "The rent I pay Franco for two days is almost as much as I pay my mom for the whole month!"

The glass doors to the restaurant opened and they were enveloped by darkness and subtle jazz from a combo at the far end. A thick wall of people stood at the bar and it appeared that every table was occupied.

Beside her, Zach said, "Behold the San Francisco meat market."

Toes don't fail me now. Marnie was very glad she'd spent the afternoon with Cecily and that Franco had taken an interest in her. She'd have to upgrade his laptop as a thank-you. Carnahan threw away computers newer than Franco's and employees got salvage rights.

While she'd been staring, Zach had spoken to the hostess who now led them through a door to another room, also with packed tables. The walls were etched mirrors that reflected the bar area and in this room, banquettes lined two walls. People must hook up at the bar and then come here to sit.

Marnie and Zach ended up near the center of the room, which made Marnie uncomfortable. More people could see her here, she thought, battling a sudden lack of self-confidence.

Earlier, she'd been nervous and had probably talked too much, but Zach hadn't complained. Then, again, he'd been very grumpy.

Nobody is paying any attention to you, she lectured herself, darting a glance around the room for reassurance.

She was anything but reassured. Everyone was looking at her. She turned wide eyes to Zach to see if he noticed, but one of the subtle overhead table lights caught him just then and gilded his hair.

Wow. And she'd always thought she was a jeans and T-shirt girl. Zach wore a white shirt under a gray crewneck sweater with black pants and looked better than the sales guys in her office, who were generally the best dressers. Still, it was the muted beam from the recessed lighting that provided the final touch and added the shadows under Zach's cheek bones. He was one good-looking man, in a craggy manly kind of way, which wasn't exactly Marnie's type. Or hadn't been. She had a feeling it was now. Especially since he seemed to be packing some brains with the brawn.

But she was beginning to understand something. It was an equation: mucho man equaled mucho woman. If she intended to go after a Zach type of man, competition was going to be fierce and she'd have to learn how to become a Zach type of woman.

She had a long way to go. Nobody was looking at her. All the women in the room had checked out Zach and the men were looking over to see what their dates saw.

Marnie couldn't believe she'd had the nerve to ask this guy for pointers. But who better, right? They had a deal, so she should get what she could out of it. She tried to relax and sat in the chair the hostess held for her, careful not to pull it too close to the table and bash into her water bra.

Keeping with the restaurant's theme, the center of the table held a bud vase crowded with sprigs of rosemary, mint and thyme. Marnie squeezed some rosemary needles to release the scent. She inhaled and smiled. "So what's lesson number one?" she asked since Zach wasn't saying anything. "My date and I have arrived at the table."

Zach nodded toward the bar in the other room. "Are you a drinker?"

He looked so good under that light. Too bad he was engaged to the Painted Ladies. "Occasionally. I don't go looking for alcohol, but I have no moral objection."

"Then your rule is that you may have one and only one alcoholic drink."

Marnie didn't need this kind of instruction. "Don't worry, I'm not going to get drunk."

Zach held up a finger. "One."

"Okay, okay."

"And keep that and anything else you drink within sight at all times. You don't want anybody putting anything in the glass that shouldn't be in there."

"Jeez, Louise! You and Franco have serious trust issues."

"Just be careful until you get your dating legs."

"Hmm." Marnie playfully stuck out her foot. "I didn't think these were so bad."

She watched Zach's gaze travel down her leg and linger at her toes. Marnie wiggled them. Zach met her eyes. "They're okay," he said. But his eyes said more. Lots more. More than Marnie was prepared to deal with. She was just joking.

Wasn't he?

She couldn't tell. She honestly couldn't tell. Her chest suddenly felt tight and it had nothing to do with the new bra. Why was it when Zach looked at her that way, it was sexy, but other guys—on the rare occasions she'd encountered the look before—made it seem like a leer?

And if Zach wasn't joking, then what was he doing letting his eyes say stuff they shouldn't? Did he know what they were saying?

As Marnie very much wished she had her one drink in front of her, the edges of Zach's mouth turned up in the barest of smiles. The rat was playing with her.

Wasn't he?

Well, she'd just be cool. She'd ignore Zach and his

sexy looks and maybe she should keep her toes to herself. "So, what about my date? Are there rules for him?"

"He may also have one drink." Zach answered as though nothing had happened.

Probably because nothing had. She was so out of her league. But that was okay. Zach was explaining the league rules.

"If he orders a second, consider it a yellow flag. Third round, you call a cab."

"Wouldn't it be better for me to ask to drive?"

Zach leveled a look at her and she parroted, "The guy drives. I don't know about that one. He shouldn't be on the road."

"No. But you won't know him well enough to take that responsibility."

"So you're saying that later—"

"I'm saying there won't be a later. You don't need to date stupid men," he decreed.

"Gotcha." Marnie withheld any comments about how many men that eliminated. "So, what do I order?"

"The 'in' thing is one of the flavored martinis."

"Ooo. What flavors are there?"

Their waitress arrived in time to overhear and began reciting. "There's the Appletini, Badgertini, Blues Martini, Butterscotch Martini—"

Zach grimaced at that one

"—Cajun Martini, Chocolate Raspberry Martini, Chocolatini, Cosmopolitan, Flirtini, Jazz Martini, Mardi Gras Martini and the Woo-Woo."

Marnie asked what was in several of them and

couldn't decide but figured Zach would order a different one and she could taste it, too. Eventually, she settled on an Appletini—vodka, apple cider and apple schnapps.

"Scotch rocks," Zach said.

"Hey, hang on a minute!" Marnie glared at him. "Why didn't you order one of the 'tinis?"

"Men don't drink those."

"Oh, please! Just look over at the bar." Marnie could see it in the mirrors. "See all the guys with martini glasses?"

Zach didn't look. "As I said, *men* don't drink those."

Marnie sat back and crossed her arms. "James Bond. Manly, manly, manly."

Zach stared down at the votive candle next to the herbs in the center of the table, then looked up at the waitress. "Martini. Dry."

The waitress hurried off.

"You didn't say shaken, not stirred," Marnie said.

"Shaking makes them cloudy. I like everything clear."

"Oh." She leaned forward. "Ya gonna let me taste it?"

Zach's gaze dropped to her mouth. He said nothing. He didn't have to.

After two seconds of silence, Marnie became aware of a warmth in her lips. What were they doing, blushing? Could lips blush?

And why didn't Zach answer? Why was he looking at her like that again? Cool. She would remain cool. Maybe it was a test. "What? Are you worried about germs? Surely the alcohol will kill them off." He hadn't seemed like the prissy type.

"No, I'm thinking about a big ole' pink lipstick print on my glass."

"Yeah, I can see where that would neutralize the masculine-enhancing effects of the martini. By the way, do try to keep up with technology. This lipstick doesn't come off."

Before she knew what he was going to do, Zach reached across the table and brushed his thumb across her lower lip. It tingled. Man, did it tingle.

He glanced at his thumb. "How about that."

Her lip still tingled. She could feel her pulse in it. "Yeah. How about that."

They stared at each other while Marnie reminded herself that Zach was just her coach. Her how-to-be-somebody-else's-girlfriend coach.

He was not for her—or rather, she was not for him. He had his Victorian houses—the most important things in his life—and she had...Barry to deal with.

Really, one teasing look and she was ready to fling herself at Zach. He probably got that a lot. Sexy man on the prowl might be his natural look. He was used to being with sexy women, she reminded herself. Sexy women who were accustomed to looks like that.

Their drinks arrived providing a much-needed distraction. With relief, Marnie immediately studied hers. It was a serene spring-green in the classic martini glass.

Zach's was sharply clear. It looked like liquid diamonds, catching the light and throwing it back, all sparkling and bright. It was the essence of cool sophistication and required a cool sophistication to drink it.

Slowly, Zach pushed his drink across the table toward her.

That's right. She'd asked for a taste. Okay. She'd wrap her fingers around that stem and tilt the rim toward her lips, making sure she glanced up at him as she did so. Cool. Sophisticated. Sexy. She'd be Jane Bond.

Mentally humming the Bond theme music, Marnie took a sip and felt an icy burn slide over her tongue. The flavor followed a moment later. "That's freaking nasty! It tastes like I'm drinking a Christmas tree!" She stared at the glass in betrayal. How could anything with "tini" in the name taste so bad? "My tongue is numb."

"That should help with the taste." Zach plucked the drink from her fingers. Looking at her from beneath his brows, he turned the rim, then tilted it to his lips in the exact spot from which Marnie had drunk and swallowed. Setting the glass on the table, he leaned back in the chair. Cool. Sophisticated. Sexy.

Annoyingly cool, sophisticated and sexy.

"So that's how it's done, right?" she asked.

"What?"

"The tasting ritual. Turning it into a little sexy man/woman thing."

He half smiled. "Was it?"

"Wasn't it supposed to be?"

"You might be overanalyzing things."

"Oh." Where was a good hole in the floor when you needed one? Marnie felt her cheeks heat. Clearly, she couldn't do cool, sophisticated and sexy. Maybe she should go for fun, fizzy and hot. Her face was already there.

Wait a minute. When had she started being embarrassed when an attractive man gave her a look like that? When was the last time an attractive man had given her a look like that?

Hmm. It had been a while, but that's why she was here. Okay. Zach was teaching her flirting. So she'd flirt until one of them cried "uncle."

And it wasn't going to be her.

6

MARNIE TOOK a cautiously experimental sip from her drink. "Ooo. Better. Much better. A nice sour zing. It makes me pucker." She did so, making a kissing sound as she separated her lips.

Zach blinked. Was she overdoing it?

"Just a suggestion, but you might want to save the advanced moves for a later date," he said.

Marnie gave him a teasing smile. "How much later?"

"When you intend to back them up."

"Oh." Marnie made a face. "That."

Yeah, everything came around to sex sooner or later, didn't it? Marnie took in Zach's widened eyes and wary expression.

"Have you got a problem with...that?" he asked cautiously.

Oh, for pity's sake. Marnie wondered if she answered "yes," he'd volunteer to cure her problem.

More likely, he'd run for the hills. She crossed her legs—his eyes followed the movement—and lifted a shoulder. "I don't think so." She sipped at her drink, noting that he was hanging on every word. "I mean it's nice, but so far I've found that it's overrated. I'm thinking there's gotta be more to it." She looked at him guilelessly over the top of her drink.

He took a gulp of his martini. Then another. Had she rattled him? Hey. He was rattled. How about that? Maybe she should try a little more rattling and see what happened. This was just for practice, right?

Right. "I've only had friend sex," Marnie continued, "that could be the problem." She smiled at him. "I just need more experience."

It was a sign of Zach's inner turmoil that he knocked back another slug of martini, then stared into the bottom of the empty glass.

"I think it's okay to be friends with your lovers, but not lovers with your friends." She smiled. "What do you think?"

"I think they're supposed to be serving martinis in oversized glasses these days." He raised both the glass and his eyebrows at their server. Then he glared at her.

"Zach?"

"What?" He snapped off the word.

"Does talking about sex make you uncomfortable?" Marnie made her eyes wide in faux sympathy.

With a look toward the bar, Zach drew a long, slow breath. "When you introduce sex as a casual topic of conversation before we've even ordered dinner, you're sending a certain message. Trust me, it's a message that will drown out anything you say afterward."

"Relax. I'm not sending the message to you."

"Yeah, I know." He looked put out, Marnie noted with delight.

"Hey, don't you think I'm doing pretty well with this flirting stuff?"

"Yeeeess." He gritted his teeth. He actually gritted his teeth. "Do you do this on all your dates?"

"Never. I swear."

"Congratulations. You're a natural."

"Really? Thanks." Marnie indulged in a little preening. "But I need more practice. I'm thinking we could be on to something here."

"And I think we can move on to something else."

Marnie wanted to spend more time on flirting, since it seemed to be so effective. If she could get to Zach, then she could get to any man.

Zach's martini arrived just then and his expression of gratitude would make a person think he'd spent the past week wandering in Death Valley.

"Oooo." Marnie made her lips pucker.

Zach stared at them as he took a largish swallow of his drink.

"Yellow flag," she said.

"What?"

Grinning, she pointed. "Drink two. Caution."

Zach cleared his throat. "And don't you forget it."

"I won't."

Just then, their server brought them hand-lettered menus which stopped her fun, mainly because Zach held the menu up like a screen between them. Marnie glanced at the entrées and snickered. "Okay, I know not to order the lobster."

He lowered the menu enough to make eye contact. "They don't have lobster."

She glanced up at him through her lashes. "It was a

joke." One he clearly didn't get. "So what are the rules?"

"There aren't any. No, wait. I'm declaring this a rule—no skipping dessert and then eating half of mine. If you want a dessert, order one."

Mr. Cranky was back. "You're not into sharing?"

"One bite. But it never stops there."

Marnie leaned her chin in her hand. "So you've got a sweet tooth."

"Maybe." Zach's gaze went to her mouth.

Marnie ran her fingers slowly up and down the stem of the martini glass. Twice. "What kind of sweets?"

He looked straight into her eyes. "Apple. Pie."

"Then you might like my drink. Wanna taste?"

They both looked at Marnie's half-filled glass and what her fingers were doing on the glass stem. Zach reached out and stilled her fingers.

Marnie was conscious of the warmth of his hand spreading up her arm. It had just been a joke, that move with the martini glass stem. She'd seen it on TV. She was pretty much trying everything to see what stuck. So far everything had. But Zach wasn't the only one affected. It was getting harder and harder to remind herself he was doing this as a favor. Sure, she'd offered him a new Web site, but she'd looked at the one he had now and, though it was very small and staid, it got the job done. He didn't need to be here.

She didn't know why her amateurish attempts at sexy flirting were working on him, but guessed that he was intrigued more by her as a "project" than as a woman.

She slithered her hand from beneath his grasp. "Hey, you should have said you wanted a taste." Remembering him turning the glass to her mouth print earlier brought a quiver to the last couple of words now, but she smiled, determined to keep it light from now on.

Zach gazed at the drink as though certain he wouldn't like it. He grimaced after an infinitesimal sip. "It's not sweet."

"It sure isn't that." Marnie casually took another sip and glanced over the menu. Keep it light. "I'm having the grilled chicken over artichoke rice. I like artichokes. What kind of foods do you like—beside sweets?"

"I don't know. Just regular food." He was back to staring at the menu.

Keeping it light did not mean allowing herself to be ignored. "What kind of regular food?"

"Food food."

"Mexican food? Chinese? Italian? Southwestern? Vegetarian? Fusion?"

Their waitress arrived then and Marnie ordered her chicken while Zach continued to stare at the menu. "Steak, rare, baked potato with the works. Caesar salad," he said.

"American food," Marnie said, drawing out the words. "Manly, artery-clogging food."

"The martini will clear it out," Zach muttered. Handing the menu to their server, he drew a breath. "Okay. Next lesson. This is idle chitchat time. You get to know him. He gets to know you. You're witty and amusing and interested and he's—"

"Grumpy?"

"Give me a break, Marnie. I've never analyzed a date before."

"Okay. Does the flirting count for the interested part while I'm being witty and amusing?"

"I meant interested in the man."

"So did I."

He threw a longing glance toward his martini glass. "Stuff about the man's life, Marnie. Forget flirting and concentrate on the conversation. As a woman, you have to take the lead. I know it's not fair, but that's just the way it is."

"Would that be because the man is having too many martinis?"

"No, it's because the man is preoccupied with thoughts of sex—will he or won't he get any and if so, how soon!" Zach stopped and lowered his voice. "So he can't carry on much of a conversation."

"I see." Marnie finished the last of her drink and thunked it down with more force than she'd intended. "So while you pretend to be interested, I'll pretend to be witty and ha-ha-ha amusing."

There was silence while Marnie tried to come up with something witty. She wished she could go back to flirting because she was much more successful with that. She shot off questions about hobbies—none. Movies—none. Current television? Didn't watch it. And books? They hadn't read any in common.

There was another protracted silence. Things were not going well in this department.

Zach exhaled. "What do you normally talk about?"

"Work. Code mistakes. Code problems. Code we've written. New software. New hardware."

"Okay. As a general rule, unless you're dating a fellow techie, avoid that stuff."

"What about fashion?" She batted her eyelashes at him. "Talk about that?"

"Uh, no."

"Good. I don't know anything about it." She looked expectantly at him. "We've covered sex, so I guess that leaves politics."

"Not yet. Save the controversial stuff for later dates."

Marnie sighed. "I'm out of ideas."

"Try travel."

"Ooo, good one. Except that I haven't traveled."

"That's why you should ask your date. Why haven't you traveled?"

"I thought I was supposed to ask the questions."

"Not all of them. You have to answer some, too."

She eyed him as their meal was served. "Are there any more rules you're going to add as we go along?"

"Probably. Now—your lack of travel?"

"Just never got around to it. I'd have to make plans and have somebody to travel with. What about you?"

"There you go. You need a little more info mixed with the questions. Let's see, I've done Europe and Greece and Italy. Italy three times. My parents took the whole family on a cruise to Mexico."

"Wow. Which was your favorite?"

"Italy. Loved Italy."

"What did you love about it?"

As he told her, Marnie was thinking that so far, the

conversation thing was pretty much what she already knew, but had never executed very well. She needed to get out more. Read more outside her field. Surf the Internet, but Marnie figured spending each and every day in front of the computer and talking only to computer people was part of her problem. Maybe most of her problem. She'd forgotten how to interact with the rest of the world.

To those outside the field, she was boring. She could see that. Just look at Zach. He was the epitome of bored. Getting him to talk was hard until she'd asked him about the house he was restoring. Then he'd started going into history and technical details, and, well, her mind had wandered. It had wandered all over his face and across his lips and slid up and down his square jaw. It had admired their reflection in the mirrors along the walls and had caught other women still looking their way.

Marnie didn't blame them.

She could see a downside to these lessons. She didn't want to attract a man less than Zach. He and his slightly antiquated but ever-so-manly rules had spoiled her.

She really liked him. He was such a sweetheart to help her like this. She had to admit that seeing him flustered when she'd flirted with him had gone a long way to negating Barry's stupid remarks. At least now, she believed what Barry had said was stupid and that there were men—terrific, manly men with a rescuing complex—who did find her attractive.

She was glad she'd rented the apartment and had gone shopping and had had her hair done and gotten

locked out and was now sitting across the table from a big, handsome guy with a tender streak.

Zach had stopped talking and was just looking at her. Oops. This wasn't good. She should have paid more attention.

"Sorry. My mind wandered," she told him.

Zach laughed. "You aren't supposed to admit that."

"I didn't know if you'd be giving a pop quiz, or anything."

"Ouch. Is that your way of saying I'm boring?"

"It's my way of saying that I wasn't paying attention because I was watching all the women watch you."

He blinked and gosh, darn it, was that a blush?

"Oh, come on," she said. "You know you're a hottie. You should be used to it by now."

"You think I'm a *hottie?*" He looked surprised.

"I can't use hottie? Stud seemed kind of, well, I don't know. Handsome is mamby-pamby. A looker sounds like I've been watching gangster movies. Good-looking is what my great-aunt would say. I could have just said 'hot,' but it's a bit direct. Cute is high-schoolish and doesn't address the jaw."

He had a peculiar expression on his face. "Jaw?"

"You have a very manly, square jaw. In a movie, you'd be the police lieutenant. You'd be the politician, you'd be the slick bad guy. You'd be the hero, the army sergeant leading his troops into battle. You'd be the sheriff in a western, the captain of the football team, the fraternity president."

"Is that good?"

She lifted a shoulder. "If that sort of person appeals to you."

His voice took on an edge. "Does it appeal to you?"

"Of course! I'm genetically programmed for it to appeal to me. A woman seeks the best male specimen to mate with. A strong square jaw implies lots of testosterone and vigorous little swimmers who'll get the job done and give a woman genetically superior children who'll have a higher chance of survival."

Zach took a sip of water, stared at her, then drank deeply. "I think I see part of your problem. When I said 'does it appeal to you,' you were supposed to answer 'yes.'"

"I thought you'd be interested in knowing that personal preference had nothing to do with you being attractive to women."

"So you're telling me I hit the genetic jackpot."

"Bingo."

Zach sat back in his chair and looked at her. Marnie looked back until she couldn't stand it anymore and had to ask, "Did I say something wrong?"

Zach opened his mouth, then closed it and shook his head.

"Then why are you looking at me that way?"

"You haven't dated many square-jawed men, have you?"

"Nope. I usually go for the brainiacs. I guess 'cause they're the most available. All the square jaws are taken."

"Marnie, you can have any man you want."

She shook her head. "Barry said I couldn't have any man and you say I can."

"We've already established that Barry is an idiot."

Marnie looked down at her plate. "Unfortunately, current evidence supports Barry's theory."

"If you need evidence, that's easy enough."

Their server arrived with the check and both Marnie and Zach reached for it at the same time.

"No," Zach said.

"I asked you for help. I should pay."

"The man pays." He didn't let go of the leather folder.

"Zach—"

"No."

Marnie relinquished her hold, but went for her purse. "At least let me—"

"No." Zach plopped his credit card into the folder.

"What if I make more money than the man?"

"Double no. He'll need to salvage his pride."

"You know, you have a lot of cavemanesque rules. Are these just rules for you, or rules for all men?"

MARNIE WAITED for his response with an I-got-you smile on her lips. Her lush, pink little lips. So sue him. They were luscious, kissable lips and Zach was human and he was going to notice them and he didn't care.

Not anymore. He'd spent the entire meal trying not to be aware of Marnie. Trying to regain control, which was a laugh because he hadn't been able to control his feelings or the situation since he'd first seen her this evening. No—to be truthful, he hadn't controlled anything since he'd seen her shivering on the balcony.

He had goals here. Things to accomplish and the disaster with Caitlin had told him that he'd better accomplish them before getting involved with anybody. Especially anybody who was still hung up on some other guy.

He was exhausted from fighting feelings he didn't expect and trying to pretend he didn't have in the first place. Anytime he relaxed a bit, he'd felt himself drawn to her as though she was the world's largest magnet and he was an iron filing. He wasn't exactly great company and rather than pout, she'd gently tried to lighten his mood. When that hadn't worked, she'd called him on it. She was no pushover. Zach liked that about her, but other men might not.

He couldn't figure Barry out. Marnie must have threatened the guy. She was probably too much woman for him. She was smart and, when she wanted to be, flat-out gorgeous. If she worked it a little more, she could be a jaw-dropper, but that wasn't her style.

He liked her style. He was so tempted by her, but Marnie was a distraction that he couldn't afford right now. It wouldn't be fair to her. She could be a case of right person, wrong time.

Time to toss this little fish back into the pond. "My rules apply to any man worth dating," he said in answer to her question.

"There are lots of rules, but you haven't really told me how to act like a girlfriend. I'm not sure what I should be doing."

"What you're doing now is fine." More than fine. Probably too fine.

"But I'm doing what I always do and so far, that hasn't been fine at all."

"You haven't dated the right men, Marnie." He waited until she met his eyes. Then he said slowly and distinctly, "You could have any man in this room. The next room, too." He'd been aware of the covert and not-so-covert looks, stares and the general checking out she'd been receiving. Hadn't she?

If he hadn't been sitting here, someone else would have been.

For a minute it looked like she might believe him, then she heaved a great sigh. "Oh, Zach. You're such a sweetie. You're trying to bolster my self-image. It's okay. Really. I just need to fine-tune my presentation."

"So you do believe you can have any man here?"

"My self-image is realistic, not stupid."

"Your self-image is blind. You need a road test. See the bar?" he asked.

"Like I could avoid it when they've so conveniently positioned the mirrors everywhere."

He slipped his credit card out of the folder and signed the receipt. "I'm going to pretend to make a phone call. I'll stay five minutes or so. I want you to walk over to the bar and order a drink."

"But you said I couldn't have more than one drink."

"I said order a drink, not drink one."

Her eyes widened. "You're trying to see if guys will hit on me?"

"I know guys will hit on you."

"But...but what do I do?"

"Trust me." Zach stood and pulled back her chair. "You won't have to do anything."

He left her at the entrance to the bar and, because of

the helpfully placed mirrors, was able to see her progress.

And did she look back at him? No. She took a couple of hesitant steps and then flipped her hair back and strode forward, confidently, maybe even eagerly. Yeah, damn it, eagerly. Very eagerly.

Zach did a little striding himself into a dark, shadowy corner near the restrooms and public phones so he could watch the action and remind himself of all the reasons why he shouldn't try very, very hard to make her forget all about Barry and go home with him. And stay for a few weeks.

Yeah, yeah. He knew it was a bad idea. That didn't seem to help, though.

Zach crossed his arms and leaned against the back wall and watched her, feeling just as strongly attracted to her as ever. He'd thought being around her would reveal some quirk or trait that would make her less attractive. Nope. Now he had a deeper attraction than before.

He wanted to touch her so much his fingertips ached. He wanted to draw her to him and lose himself in her softness. He wanted to feel her hair sliding over his skin.

And he wanted to kiss those pink lips.

And he wasn't going to because it wouldn't be fair to either of them. Marnie had been upfront about wanting a relationship. She was at that point in her life.

He wasn't. Breaking up with Caitlin had hurt. Everyone had focused on her and how unfair he'd been. No one had thought he might have been hurt, too, or if they did, they'd thought he'd deserved to be hurt.

So, he'd learned the lesson. Business first, then a relationship.

Marnie reached the outer line of people, those who just had drinks served and those who were talking to them.

She slid past one cluster and Zach watch the heads swivel. Male first, then female. The females swiveled back. The male heads did not.

She parted the sea of people like a jigsaw through plaster.

Zach wanted to hit somebody. Maybe several somebodies.

A couple of men murmured to each other as they checked out Marnie. It was probably a good thing he couldn't lip read.

She reached the counter and the sea closed around her. Zach had to move in order to watch what was happening. Not that he needed to see to know that men were offering to buy her a drink, giving her worn-out come-on lines that would seem fresh and flattering to her.

A head or two scanned the crowd, clearly looking for him. They'd been watching her for a while, he thought morosely.

Zach made himself unclench his fists. The world had discovered his hidden treasure and he didn't like it. What had he thought would happen when he'd encouraged her to go to the bar?

Exactly that. He just hadn't expected to mind so much.

There was a mirror over the bar. In the reflection, he saw the wolves circling.

Marnie's head was moving back and forth as she tried to carry on a conversation with everyone. She looked so pretty. So fresh. So unjaded and unspoilt. Her cheeks were flushed and she was holding one of those barbaric faux martini drinks that exactly matched her blush.

She touched the drink to her lips and Zach guessed she was tasting it. He was curious to see if she'd actually drink it—or the other two that had appeared on the bar in front of her. Either she hadn't seen them yet, or she didn't realize they'd been ordered for her.

She threw back her head and laughed and one of the men touched her shoulder.

Zach straightened. He hadn't addressed touching. He should have addressed touching.

But Marnie wasn't a child, she was a woman—albeit an inexperienced one. Maybe not inexperienced so much as not used to all the attention.

And maybe not so inexperienced, either, he thought as he watched her turn so the man had to drop his hand. Then she crossed her legs so that he couldn't get any closer.

That left her back open...was that an elbow he saw?

Okay, inexperienced was the wrong word. Rusty. That was it. She was just rusty.

And getting unrusty remarkably fast.

Five minutes went by. Then five more. Marnie was having the time of her life. Three men jockeyed for position around her. Two women several seats down sent her venomous looks. He hoped Marnie saw, but then again, Marnie didn't seem like the type of woman who'd enjoy making other women jealous.

He hoped this would give her the confidence to confront Barry and do whatever she was going to do about him.

It wasn't his business and he wouldn't make it his business. He couldn't. For the first time, Zach resented the grueling work schedule he'd set for himself.

He let five more minutes go by. Five more tortuous minutes while he reevaluated his life and what was important to him. He should leave. Just leave.

But he couldn't abandon her. He'd brought her, he'd take her home.

He swallowed. Her home. Her temporary home.

Not his home, which was a tiny studio in a undesirable area of San Francisco. By choice, he reminded himself. All he needed was a place to sleep and the ability to plow as much as he could into his company. Or to be technically accurate, the restoration arm of Renfro Construction. He'd like to make it an independent company, but not enough to absorb the business hassles of doing so. Not yet. Maybe not—

One man was acting a little too familiar with Marnie—trying to cut her away from the rest of the pack. He had his arm across her shoulder and was leaning down to speak close to her ear.

Zach had had enough. If Marnie wanted to go off with some jerk, she'd have to come back and do it on her own time. He had no intention of watching. He couldn't.

Zach stormed toward the bar, consciously slowing as he approached and made his way toward Marnie.

"Hey, babe, ready to go?" he asked when he finally got within earshot.

He'd caught her laughing at something somebody had said, so when she turned her head, her eyes crinkled and her lips were parted. "Zach!"

He lost his breath and felt light-headed. She was happy to see him and he was happy to be seen.

He drew his arm across her shoulders. That's all he meant to do, but once he touched her, the control he'd wrestled with all evening evaporated and left him with unchecked desire. He forgot about his work and his good intentions and that he was supposed to be giving Marnie dating pointers.

His gaze fastened on her mouth and he leaned down and kissed her, his lips touching hers at last.

He kissed her because she talked too much. He kissed her because she'd been driving him nuts all evening. He kissed her to show all the other men that she was leaving with him. He kissed her because he wanted to.

And he kissed her because he had to.

For a moment, her lips were soft and warm, with a tang of apple, then they hardened in surprise.

What they didn't do was kiss him back. Zach figured he was pretty much toast.

He broke the kiss and met her gaze, unsure of her reaction.

Marnie blinked twice then chirped, "Hi!" Looking around she continued, "Everybody, this is Zach. Zach—" she waved around "—this is everybody." And she giggled.

Zach hadn't figured her for a giggler. He sent a look

around and received a grudging acknowledgment from the men. The women were more enthusiastic.

"I'm having just the best ole time, Zach!" Marnie was still chirping like a birdbrain.

"Ready to go?" he asked her at the same time he took hold of her upper arm because, after all, it was a rhetorical question.

"Ooo. Am I ready to go, Zach?"

"Yes." If he didn't know better, he'd think she'd consumed all the drinks lined up in front of her.

Slithering off the bar stool in a way Zach found totally unnecessary, Marnie cooed, "Bye, guys." Then she waggled her fingers and giggled again.

He wouldn't have been surprised if she'd skipped out the door.

Instead, she docilely wrapped herself around his arm and walked outside with him.

That should have warned him, but he'd been distracted by the giggling and the bad Mae West imitation, not to mention kissing her.

In fact, he wanted to kiss her again. Longer. In private. As soon as possible.

The instant they were through the door, Marnie pointedly withdrew her arm. "Zach?" She drew out his name and made it all sugary.

Maybe she liked the kiss as much as he did.

"What the hell was that?"

Or maybe not. "It was time to leave."

"I'm talking about the way we left."

Nope. She hadn't liked the kiss. Well, sure, he hadn't planned on kissing her at all, but now that he had, Zach was toying with the idea of telling her he could do better, when she ranted on.

"You said you'd be gone five minutes. That was the longest five minutes I ever lived through. What was it? Fifteen? Twenty?"

"Seventeen and a half," he mumbled.

"So you sent me to the bar, watched me do exactly what you wanted me to do, then you go and get all territorial. Good grief, is it some square-jawed guy thing? Did you forget who you were with? I mean, I collected business cards!" She fanned them right in front of his face. "After you had your macho attack, I might as well...well..." She tossed them into the air.

The wind scattered them as the valet arrived with Zach's car. One landed on his shoe. He kicked it off.

Marnie climbed into the car with a flash of leg and toenails and slammed the door before either he or the valet could shut it.

The problem with apologizing, Zach thought as he walked around to the driver's side and got into the car, was that he wasn't sorry.

He slammed the door with equal force. They both stared straight ahead. "I'm not sorry," Zach said.

"What are you not sorry for?"

"I am not sorry for getting you away from those jackals." He glanced at her. "And for the record, I'm not sorry I kissed you."

"Well, why would you be? You got to swagger in, mark your territory and walk off with the prize. Didja get a good testosterone buzz out of that, Zach?"

She completely missed the point. The kiss was the point.

"The testosterone buzz came from the kiss." Ha. Hardball. See how she handled that.

He put the car into gear and drove off.

"You got a buzz off that puny little thing? Oh, poor Zach. It really has been a while, hasn't it?"

He nearly ran the red light. "You appeared to be in distress, so I used the most efficient way to get you out of there."

"Distress, huh? What, uh, what kind of distress?"

Zach warmed to his explanation. "You—you were flushed. And you giggled. A lot. That's a sign of nerves."

"I thought it was a sign of flirting."

"I didn't like you flirting," he mumbled.

"Then why did you put me in a flirting situation?"

Why was she making this all complicated? "So you would see that men find you attractive."

She smiled in a way he did not like at all. "Yeah. That was cool. It was like magic, or something. I mean it's never happened before. And it was so easy—" She broke off abruptly. "Zach, those weren't friends of yours, were they?"

"No."

"You didn't pay them off, did you?"

"Why would I do that?"

"That is exactly something you'd do to make me feel good."

Zach considered. "Nah. I wouldn't because you'd eventually find out and we'd have a big argument."

"We're having a big argument now and you didn't pay anyone."

"This isn't a big argument, this is a difference in philosophy."

"And that would be the philosophy of...?"

"The philosophy of you not being taken advantage of."

"What did you think I was going to do? Go off with one of them?"

Zach slid a look toward her then away.

"You did!" Marnie laughed.

At least she was laughing now and not giggling. "How was I supposed to know what you'd do? It was a new experience for you. It might have gone to your head."

"I wouldn't have left with anyone. At least, not tonight."

His foot twitched on the accelerator.

"You know, I don't get it. I don't look that different, do I?"

She expected him to actually answer a no-win question?

"Do I?"

She did expect him to answer. "Yes and no," he finally said. "But it doesn't take much. A lot of it is attitude."

"That's what Barry said." She was quiet for a moment. "But the only attitude I had when I went up there was how to get past the people to the bar and what to do when I got there. And trying to look like I'd done it a hundred times before."

"Part of your appeal is that you don't look like you've done it a hundred times before."

"Hmm. Well. I still think there's something more to it."

When she found out, Zach hoped she'd tell him.

MARNIE HAD BEEN doing just fine until he kissed her. How was she supposed to keep herself from going gaga over him if he kissed her?

It was so not fair that he could just kiss people for the heck of it and not have to deal with a heart pounding so loud it drowned out all other sound. Or the suddenly moist palms. Or having to remember to breathe. Or think.

Honestly, Marnie had no idea how long he'd kissed her before her brain had begun to function again. It was unexpected and shocking and wonderful.

Fortunately, before she embarrassed both of them by kissing him back, her brain had begun sending her faint signals asking for a reality check. So, she hadn't kissed him back, though she'd wanted to.

He wasn't teasing her on purpose, but it still made her mad. He should know the effect he had on women.

She liked Zach. A lot. But honestly, even if he weren't so into his work, he was too much man for her. A man like Zach demanded a feminine woman. Marnie would never be able to hold his interest and being the kind of woman who could was way too much effort to sustain permanently. It was fun for a while, but in the end, Marnie guessed she was just cut out to be a pal, after all.

By the time they arrived at her apartment, she was

exhausted from engaging in witty, if she did say so herself, pal-like conversation during the drive.

Zach parked across the street where he usually parked his Bronco so he could walk her to the door without double parking.

"You could have just dropped me off," she said.

Zach threw her a withering look. "A man walks his date to the door and sees her safely inside. You don't get dropped off unless it's pouring rain and that's the best way to keep you dry. Even then, he should wait until you're inside."

"If you say so."

He looked down at her as they crossed the street. "Don't tell me you've let the brainiacs get away with dropping you off."

"I live in Pleasant Hill, remember? I take BART home."

"They don't drive you home?"

She shook her head.

"Tell me they ride with you, then."

"Usually I just catch a bus from wherever we are to the nearest BART terminal." She hadn't had too many formal dates in the past several years. Mostly it was an impromptu movie or dinner. "My usual crowd isn't into formality."

They'd reached the bottom of the steps. Marnie saw Franco's silhouette behind the curtains.

"Marnie." Zach touched her upper arm stopping her before she climbed the steps. "If you don't value yourself, then your dates won't value you, either. Promise me that at the very least, you will insist on being escorted to the BART terminal. And if it's past ten, that they ride with you or drive you all the way home. I don't care how far away it is." There was true concern in his expression.

"Okay." Marnie liked that he cared enough to be concerned about her. A warmth spread throughout her middle leaving all sorts of warm fuzzy feelings in its wake.

They stared at each other for several long moments before Zach cleared his throat and stared down at his shoes. "And um, I don't want you falling for that old it's-so-far-why-don't-you-spend-the-night line, either."

Too late. But she'd only fallen for it once. "I won't." She grinned. "Unless I want to."

Something flashed in his eyes but was quickly gone.

"Good night, Zach," she said softly. "And thanks."

His gaze dropped to her mouth.

He wants to kiss me. Yes, but would he? Just when she was about to sway forward on her toes, Zach took a half step backward.

To hide her disappointment, Marnie smiled determinedly and stuck out her hand.

She could see the relief on his face as he shook it. Good move on her part. The last thing she wanted was a pity kiss.

Marnie ran lightly up the steps, conscious of Zach watching her. As she opened the door, she turned around and smiled a last goodbye at him.

He stood looking up at her, strong and silent, his hands shoved in his pockets, the streetlight picking out the glints in his hair.

Marnie gripped the door handle so tightly the embossed decoration made an impression on her palm.

But not as deep as the impression Zach had made on her heart.

7

Yesterday, the skirt performed most satisfactorily. It's possible that it has some effect on the wearer as well. M. was remarkably docile about my suggestions to her appearance.

It was quite a successful transformation. Though I am leaning toward writing the Legend of the Skirt *as a play, simply for ease of getting it performed, I am tempted by film because the facial expressions have been priceless. I fear I shall have to invest in a digital camera because I do not want to miss another such display as Mr. R. put on when he first saw M.*

However, something happened between them last night and M., who has been very forthcoming up to this point, has become strangely reticent. They did not kiss each other good-night. There was an awkward handshake that puzzled me. Not even a social kiss near the cheek... Clearly, there has been a development to which I am not privy. Yet.

Marnie had to get over Zach right now. Immediately. She was headed for hurt if she didn't.

Franco inadvertently helped by making her buy a new coat.

"An all-weather trench," he suggested. "I can't believe you don't own one. How have you survived?"

"With a folding umbrella," Marnie had grumbled.

Still she'd dutifully bought a black trench coat, though Franco had said she could have a khaki one if it matched her stupid color swatches.

No, she sighed, they weren't stupid. They were actually helpful, if you liked shopping, which she didn't, except that it apparently got results.

Marnie was in a store near the Carnahan building. She'd been in several shops and she'd bought the black coat, even without Franco's preapproval. He'd said that even she couldn't choose a wrong trench coat. She also bought some slacks because she'd decided that she was getting too comfortable in jeans, and now she was looking for a black skirt like the one she'd borrowed from him.

No luck. She'd tried on several and they just didn't have the same rich feel when the fabric swished against her legs. In fact, they didn't swish well at all.

She gave up on the skirts and bought a pair of walking shoes that weren't nearly as much fun as the backless heels she'd bought the other day, but were more practical.

Using her swatches, she bought two more tops, one with spaghetti straps and a sparkly thread running through it that she didn't know if she would ever have the nerve to wear in public. Maybe under something. Which meant she had to find the something and she really ought to have Franco's advice about that.

Truthfully, even after all the attention in the bar last night, Marnie was a little down. This morning, Zach hadn't been at the site when she'd walked by. And she'd left off her hat and let her hair whip all around and had worn lipstick and everything...and she didn't even get a second look from his construction workers. She figured he'd read them the riot act about hassling women until just before turning the corner, she heard a whistle. Looking back, she saw the same two blond women.

And so she arrived at work with her hair all tangled for nothing.

She'd combed it, refreshed her lipstick and walked the long way around to her computer, but nobody commented on her changed appearance. Barry hadn't looked up when she'd passed by his office and Marnie hadn't said anything.

And now it was lunchtime and she didn't have time to eat because she had to shop. Honestly, she needed some positive reinforcement here.

Yeah, sure, Zach had played macho and had kissed her, but as she kept reminding herself, it hadn't meant anything. He was showing off in front of the other men.

But she'd liked that kiss, short as it was. Really liked it. She hadn't even minded the faint taste of martini because behind it was Zach. She liked the take-charge feel of his lips, compared to other kisses she'd had.

Had Zach liked the kiss? Even a little bit? He hadn't kissed her good-night, even though Marnie had expected at least a peck on the cheek. Maybe he knew she'd waylay his lips if they got anywhere near hers.

Maybe that's why they'd awkwardly shaken hands good-night. Like a business deal. Because that was what they had after all. A business deal.

Speaking of which, it was Marnie's turn to keep her side of the deal. Tomorrow, she planned to borrow the killer digital camera from work and take pictures of the house for the Web site. That would reassure Zach that she remembered the business aspect of their relationship.

Did she want it to be more? Sure. Did she think that was going to happen? Unfortunately, no. Not with her and not with anybody else, either. Zach had been pretty clear about the importance of those houses to him and what he was willing to sacrifice—namely, a relationship. The situation didn't exactly lend itself to a hot and heavy romance. Not the kind she was after, anyway.

Marnie was supposed to be smart. And if she was smart, she'd remember that and move on.

Though it would be nice to have something concrete to move on from....

No. No more time-wasting men. She'd learn what she could from Zach and be happy she'd had the opportunity. She would be happy. Very happy. Deliriously happy...

She wondered if he'd like her in that sparkly top.

ZACH HADN'T EXPECTED to see Marnie before next Monday. He didn't want to wait until next Monday—he didn't want to wait until tomorrow. He hadn't seen her yesterday and that was bad enough.

In his mind, he replayed their last moments together, when she'd run up the stairs, showing off her legs and doing it very effectively. She'd stopped and turned back to smile down at him and in his pockets, his hands had fisted with the effort to keep himself from running after her. He'd almost kissed her good-night and was still feeling the strain of holding back. It was a good thing he hadn't kissed her, but good for whom, he couldn't say. And then she'd stood in the doorway and a knot had lodged in his throat. He'd swallowed, hard, and thankfully hadn't been required to speak.

He'd thought time away from her would help, but it hadn't. This afternoon, he was thinking about trying to come up with an excuse to see her on Sunday, but he'd just ripped off the old facade on the fireplace and had discovered fine white marble beneath. Even better, antique Delft tiles of ships decorated each corner. They predated the house by more than a hundred years, so the original owners must have brought them from Holland. Zach hoped the discovery would sway the current owners into continuing the project. He'd also been able to peel away a hundred years of wallpaper to find enough of the original Victorian paper to copy. He was carefully removing a playing-card-sized piece when a feminine voice said, "Hey there."

Marnie.

He jerked and ripped the paper.

"I didn't mean to startle you," she said, stepping into the room. He barely recognized her. She looked sleek and elegant in a long, black coat and black pants. She carried an impressive looking digital camera. "I thought I'd stop by on my way home and get some pictures of this house for your Web site." She stared down at the piece of paper he held. "Is ripping that a bad thing?"

"It's, uh, the original wallpaper." Normally, he'd be beyond angry, but he only felt vaguely disappointed.

There was still enough to copy. It must be the Marnie effect.

"Gee, it sure is ugly. Brown and mustard? How depressing."

"There's red in there, too."

"Yeah. It looks like dried blood."

Zach stared at the paper, really seeing it for the first time. It was ugly. Why was Marnie the first person to point that out? Or was she the first person he'd actually listened to?

She tucked a piece of hair behind her ear. He liked that she had stopped clipping it to her skull the way she used to.

"What were you going to do with such a small piece?" she asked.

"I work with a company that can duplicate it."

She made a face. "Why would anyone want to duplicate that?"

"Because it's the original," he repeated.

"Just goes to show you that bad taste spans the ages." She knelt down and focused her camera. "Do you duplicate a lot of ugly wallpaper?"

"It's not all ugly." But a lot of it was, now that he thought about it. And why would the original owners go to all the trouble of bringing antique tiles from their homeland and then not use the blue and white color scheme?

"If you offer that service, then we'll put it on your Web site." She smiled at him. "Now, let's have some action shots. Look like you're restoring something. Use tools."

Zach picked up a putty knife.

"No. Big tools. They look more impressive."

"Marnie..."

She lowered the camera. "You're busy, huh?"

He had been. Now getting the wallpaper off didn't seem so urgent. "It's almost quitting time." As though he ever paid attention to the time when he worked. More of the Marnie effect. But was it a good or bad effect?

"So now is an okay time for pictures?"

"Sure."

"Good. Go work the saw. You look really good using the saw."

He couldn't stop the smile. Must be a good effect.

Shoving the old wallpaper into his jeans pocket, he walked over to the jigsaw and picked up a wood scrap. He set it on the table and put on the safety glasses. Without turning on the saw, he positioned it and posed. "How's this?"

"Hmm," Marnie said from behind her camera. "Take off your shirt."

"What?" Zach straightened and ripped off the safety glasses.

"Kidding."

She hadn't taken down the camera so he couldn't see her eyes. "Seriously, turn on the saw. We need action—flying woodchips or something."

Zach put down the saw and whipped off his outer shirt so the fabric couldn't get caught.

"Ooo, yeah, baby. Flex those biceps."

She surprised a laugh out of him. "Marnie!"

Marnie looked up from the camera. "Not kidding." Waggling her eyebrows, she focused again.

Zach had never been self-conscious about his body before. It did what he asked of it. In return, he watched the weekend beers and occasionally fed it veggies.

But Marnie liked it, and he liked that she liked it.

He turned on the saw and tried to avoid cutting off his thumb as he flexed. Maybe he should ask Marnie just what kind of Web site she was used to creating.

Zach had intended to make random cuts in the wood, but once he started, he impulsively cut the letter *M*, complete with curlicue gingerbread edges.

He forgot about Marnie and her camera until he finished, turned off the saw and blew sawdust off the *M*. "Souvenir." He handed it to her.

Her camera was slung over her shoulder and her arms had been crossed in front of her until she reached out to take the *M*.

"Wow." She turned it around and touched the edges, studying the piece with a thoroughness that pleased Zach.

"You weren't taking pictures."

"I took lots of pictures. You spent five minutes making this."

Had he? "It didn't seem that long."

"I could tell." Marnie pushed some buttons on the camera. "Take a look."

Zach peered at a square-inch sized preview pane on the back of the camera. Pictures flashed by each second. Closeups of him. His face. His eyes through the safety goggles.

"This is my face. I thought you wanted my biceps."

"I did, and I got a couple of your muscles, but the

expression on your face was..." She shook her head. "You love your work. It shows."

What could he say? He did.

"Hey," she said. "I'd like to get before and afters while you're doing this house, if that's okay. And I was wondering, do you have a list of houses you've restored? I want to have a page with pictures of those, too."

"What are you doing Sunday? I'll drive you around and you can take pictures." He practically fell over himself grabbing the opportunity to spend time with her. "We can make a day of it. Have a picnic." A picnic? Where had that come from?

But when he saw Marnie's face light up, he didn't care how he sounded or where the ideas had originated. He was only glad that he was going to get to see her again.

"I INSIST you spend Sunday night here."

Marnie had stopped by to show Franco her coat after taking Zach's pictures. "But, Franco, it's not my regular day."

"It's my day and I'm offering it to you. In exchange, you'll tell me everything about how things go with Mr. Renfro on Sunday."

Marnie gave him an exasperated look. "Franco, you need to get a life."

"I have a life and it happens to be deeply entwined with other lives." He placed a hand over his heart—the other hand held the two leashes of the dogs he walked in the evenings. "I am an actor and a writer. I must observe to create."

"But I'm not very interesting."

"Marnie, you are a woman in the midst of a major life change. You are intensely interesting."

Was she in the midst of a major life change? If so, what was she changing into? If—when—Barry ate his words, what would she do then? Find somebody to be a girlfriend to, she guessed without enthusiasm. Naturally, she thought of Zach at this point and fingered the wooden *M* in her pocket. He hadn't sanded it—she wouldn't let him—so sharp edges pricked her fingers. Just a little reminder that losing her heart to him would hurt, too.

MARNIE WISHED she'd brought the wooden *M* with her on Sunday because she really needed the reminder. She'd been talking to Zach on her way to and from work all week and the more she was around him, the more she wanted to be around him.

And then came Sunday. It was a relaxed, casual day and Marnie was dressed in her old jeans, with the turquoise sweater set which made her part new Marnie and part old Marnie.

As a reward, she got to see the genuine Zach, the Zach when he wasn't on the job or giving her dating pointers.

She liked this side of him, too, liked how proud he was of his past projects and how he enjoyed showing them to her. She shared his growing enthusiasm as the morning wore on. He talked—mostly about his business—but it offered Marnie a glimpse into his life. She was fascinated by everything that was involved in restoration work and how it differed from renovation.

But enough was enough and Marnie knew she was reaching her architectural saturation point.

They were in front of the sixth Painted Lady that he'd restored and Zach was explaining in exquisite detail the challenges he'd overcome to make it look the way it did now. And as usual, Marnie was looking at him and not at the house, when she had the revelation.

Zach had been pointing out gingerbread trim—which he carefully explained was different on each of his houses—and he'd looked back at her, his face glowing. Glowing. And Marnie knew in that moment that he'd never look at a woman that way.

And she also knew that she wanted to be looked at that way.

"I had to talk the owners into adding the fourth color, but that dark purple adds shading and definition. You didn't know that was purple, did you?"

Marnie obediently shook her head.

"Looks like shadows, right?"

She nodded.

"Look over there—see that woodwork beneath the eaves?"

Marnie nodded again, having learned that Zach on a roll didn't want to have an actual conversation.

"It's not wood!" He grinned back at her over his shoulder and Marnie impulsively took a picture of him with the house in the background.

She hadn't had time to focus or frame the shot, but it was his expression she was going for.

He was in love with this house. He was in love with all of them. And he was committed to them and all the houses that would come after them. There was no room for commitment to anything or anyone else.

She was wasting her time if she thought otherwise.

"That's called 'trompe l'oeil,'" Zach said. "From the edge of the window on, it's just a painted design. There wasn't room for the actual gingerbreading. And you wouldn't have known unless I pointed it out, would you?"

Marnie shook her head again. This was a different Zach than he'd been at Seasonings. That Zach had been in-your-face macho attractive. And it had worked for her because she was in her ultrafeminine mode.

But she'd toned down today and so had Zach. He seemed younger, happier, and his enthusiasm was contagious. She couldn't imagine this Zach with a martini.

She wondered how this Zach kissed.

He continued to admire his handiwork. "I come back by here every few months to check on the paint job and touch it up if I have to."

"Wow. I didn't realize trompe l'oeil was so high-maintenance."

"It's not."

Something about the way he said it prompted Marnie to ask, "Do you offer, like, a maintenance contract for the owners? Is that something to put on the Web site?"

Zach looked surprised. "I wouldn't charge for that!"

"Zach!" Marnie couldn't believe him. Free lifetime

maintenance. What a bargain. She would not put that on the Web site.

"I want it to stay looking perfect."

And Marnie had thought she was a perfectionist. But she'd never once been tempted to revisit one of her projects and tweak it for free.

"I loved this house."

"You love all your houses," Marnie said.

"Yeah. I hate the thought of giving them up—"

"Because you apparently don't."

He grinned. "Just this one. But once they're finished, another house comes along and I get involved in it."

"And you fall in love again." These Painted Ladies were his girlfriends. While he was with them, he carried on an intense affair, but when they were able to stand on their own, he let them go and stayed friends.

"I wouldn't call it falling in love...." He smiled. "Okay, maybe a little."

"Maybe a lot," Marnie murmured. "Are you sure you wouldn't just like to buy one for yourself one day?"

"Of course! Some day I will. When I find the right one."

Well, there it was, as though she needed any more proof. Zach was a classic commitment phobe—but they'd always be friends. She could just see all his ex-girlfriends calling him when they had car problems or the sink backed up or something. And Zach would help them because that's the kind of man he was.

It was hard to resent a man who was so good, but Marnie's dad had been like that and she knew the flip side. The man who always volunteered to coach and teach Sunday school and cover for people at work never found time for his own family.

People always told Marnie how lucky she was, but how would she know? Her dad had never been around much for her. And now he was gone.

Maybe that's why she was drawn to Zach; she knew his type. But she was no longer a little girl waiting for her turn with her daddy. She was a grown woman and whoever she hooked up with was going to have to put her first.

They headed back to Zach's Bronco, which, by the way, Marnie felt Caitlin, Zach's former fianceé, had been quite right in despising. The cracked vinyl seats gouged the back of her legs even through her jeans.

"You've been quiet today," he said.

"And you've been very talkative."

"Sorry about that." He didn't sound sorry, but Marnie thought the apology unnecessary anyway.

"You hungry?" he asked.

"Yes." She was ready for a break from the houses. They were beautiful and exquisitely restored, but...was it possible to be jealous of an inanimate object?

"Come on. I've got a spot for lunch picked out and on the way, you can see my dream project. Everytime I finish one house, I contact the owners and let them know I'm available." He laughed. "It's a huge home that needs help. I could turn it into a showplace B and B."

Marnie thought she could stand one more house, but when Zach pulled to the curb in front of a huge jumble of a place way up on a hill, she squinted skeptically.

"Isn't it great?" he asked.

"It's...big."

"Yeah, I know. It would take me years to do it up right, but man, I'd sure like the chance."

He drove on as Marnie thought that if she were the owners, she wouldn't want to wait years.

Unfortunately, Zach took her to Alamo Square and the park overlooking postcard row, the famous scene of six Painted Ladies with the San Francisco skyline in the background. He started to tell her about them, starting with the Shannon-Kavanaugh House which anchored the row.

Marnie obscured the view by marching in front of him, taking his face in her hands and saying, "Zach!"

"What?" He looked baffled.

"Food now. Architecture later." She dropped her hands, conscious of a pleasing roughness against her fingertips.

"Sorry." He gave her a rueful smile. "I get carried away."

Adorably carried away. "I can see that. Anyway, I wanted to talk to you about your Web site." He walked over to the Bronco without saying anything, so Marnie went on. "I've been working on it. I've got the entry page and the flash intro done, but I'll probably change the pictures. After today, I'm going to add a page with your business philosophy and maybe some history of the 1906 earthquake and the surviving Victorians. I can list links and reference books, if you know of any good ones. It'll be stuff so that clients can know you and how you operate. It'll reassure them," she added when she couldn't tell if Zach was paying attention or not.

"Sounds good."

He'd dragged lunch out of his Bronco. Marnie had visions of a romantic plaid blanket, a wicker basket filled with wine, cheese, French bread and fruit. But what Zach spread on the ground was a used drop cloth, which he assured her had no wet paint on it, and two box lunches from a delicatessen. Inside, Marnie found a smoked turkey sandwich, a pickle, a pack of sour cream and onion potato chips and an oatmeal raisin cookie. Zach handed her a bottle of water.

Marnie twisted the top on the water bottle and sighed. If she'd wanted romance, she should have taken care of the details herself. If she had, the cookie would have been chocolate chip and not something harboring raisins.

"About the rest of your Web site," she continued. "Do you charge consulting fees?"

Zach shook his head.

"You probably should. I can see an initial evaluation for free, but if you do anything more extensive, you should be compensated."

"I don't want to do that."

"You could deduct it from the total cost if they go with you."

"No, Marnie." His voice held a finality that told her he wasn't going to be amenable to many changes.

So she wouldn't tell him when she changed things. "These pictures are going to be great on the site. I'll bet you'll double your business."

He leaned on an elbow and stared at postcard row. "I don't need for it to double. I have plenty of work now."

"Then you should be charging more."

Marnie took a bite of sandwich and nearly choked at Zach's forceful "No!"

"It's more important to me to save these old buildings," he continued at a lesser volume.

"Okay." Don't argue. Don't get involved.

She was afraid she was already involved.

Get uninvolved. Zach was Zach, and he wasn't going to change. She could hang around and make herself miserable competing for his attention the way she'd competed for her father's, or save herself a fortune in therapy bills, acknowledge the pattern and break it.

Drat it all, anyway.

"I think I'm ready to confront Barry," she said abruptly.

Zach coughed and took a long swallow of water. Marnie watched his Adam's apple bob up and down. He was the only man in the world with a sexy Adam's apple.

"You think you're ready after one lesson?" he asked.

"I didn't have any trouble at the bar. I ruled at the bar."

"So how do you plan to confront this Barry guy?"

Zach sat up and swiveled away from his beloved Victorians. Marnie had his complete attention. Imagine that.

"I..." How did she plan to get Barry to notice her?

She should have come up with a plan before bringing up the subject.

"Have you seen him at work lately?" Zach asked.

"Not really. Not up close." Barry probably felt guilty after the Deli Dally incident.

"So what are you going to do? Stop by his office and say, 'Look at me. I'm a girlfriend'?"

"I haven't got that far yet." Marnie picked the raisins out of her cookie.

"And after that, what? Wait for him to say, 'I was wrong. You're one hot babe'?" He seemed awfully interested.

"I'd take that." Marnie gave up on the cookie and rested her chin on her knees. "But the idea is for him to ask me to Tarantella. That would say it all."

"And if he did, you'd turn him down, right?" Zach gazed intently at her.

What was with him? "No, because asking me out isn't enough."

"What do you mean it's not enough?"

"He wouldn't know if I was girlfriend material or not unless I went out with him."

Zach looked off toward the trees in the park—not at the houses, she noticed. "Can we dispense with the phrase 'girlfriend material' and call it like it is? You just want him to want you so you can reject him. This is exactly what I told you would happen."

He looked so disgusted that Marnie was stung into defending herself. "No, you said I wouldn't reject him."

Zach gathered up their picnic remains. "Will you?"

Marnie was irritated with him so she snapped back, "What does it matter to you?"

He gave her a long look. "It doesn't, I guess."

8

M. AND MR. R. have been out all day. M. did not wear the skirt. Must learn of any new developments.

FRANCO POUNCED. "Tell all." He grabbed for his ever-present notebook.

Coming in after a day of tramping around San Francisco, Marnie wasn't in a mood to be pounced on. "There's not much to tell."

"Trouble in paradise," Franco mouthed as he wrote.

"There's no paradise," Marnie grumbled.

"You like Mr. Renfro."

Marnie met Franco's eyes, then looked away.

He hooted delightedly. "You *love* Mr. Renfro!"

"No." She'd better not. "Mr. Renfro loves his work. I can't compete with his work and I'm not going to try." She looked defiantly at Franco.

"You may not have to try very hard."

"Franco..." Marnie slumped on the bottom step. "I'm working on his Web site so he took me around to photograph some of the houses he's done. You should have heard him. He went on and on and on."

"He does do that."

"Then in the afternoon, we went by the construction

company to get a brochure and some pictures of other restoration projects. His dad and brother run Renfro Construction and it's huge. And they were in the office working on a Sunday afternoon and Zach couldn't get out of there fast enough."

"He hates his family?" Franco asked quickly.

"Stop drooling. He adores his family and they seemed perfectly nice. I got the impression that they subsidize him so he can do his thing with the Victorians. No, he just hates working in an office."

Franco pursed his lips and drew lines through something he'd written.

"Franco, not everyone in the world is dysfunctional."

"But it's so much more interesting when they are." He bounced his pencil eraser—Marnie tried not to notice that it was a pink star—on his notebook.

"Actually, now that I think about it, I'm feeling sorta dysfunctional, myself."

"How?" Franco's pencil was poised, star quivering. "Your inner self and your outer self no longer match? Your mother hates your new look? You are ready to denounce society's preoccupation with outer beauty by appearing in public without clothes and makeup?"

"Franco!"

"Just in case you hadn't thought of it. It would make a great scene."

Marnie might be worried, if she thought he had a chance of selling his script. "I like Zach. I really do. More than I should, if you must know."

"And I must." Franco was nearly vibrating with fervor.

"I'm ready for a family."

Franco sighed.

"Zach isn't."

"Of course, he is. The man fairly drips family."

Marnie squeezed her eyes shut. "Then he'll have to make some changes to convince me." She opened her eyes and managed a smile. "Even though he's not right for me, it feels weird asking him to help me attract another man. So, I just want to show Barry he was wrong, then move on from both of them."

"Hmm." Franco wrote that down. "I'm sensing a plot point. What's tomorrow's lesson?"

"We're going to a sports bar where Barry and the guys hang out. Zach's going to show me some new moves."

Franco gasped. "May I come?"

"*No!*" Franco in a sports bar?

Looking wounded, Franco set aside his notebook. "I can trade you a piece of advice for details on your evening."

Didn't she end up telling him everything anyway? "Sure. Why not?"

"Marnie."

She looked up at him. His eyes were kind and knowing and she had the sense that what he was going to tell her was very wise and she should pay attention.

"Remember that everything Mr. Renfro tells you about flirting or attracting a man will work on him."

"But I don't want anything to work on him."

Franco said nothing, but reached for his notebook. She hated it when he did that.

"IT WOULD HELP your image if you weren't checking the door every fifteen seconds," Zach said. He wished Marnie's Barry would walk into the sports bar so they could get this over with.

Sunday had blown him away, and then to find out that what Barry thought still mattered to her had stunned him. And it affected his work today. He'd always been able to lose himself in his work. Until Marnie had come along.

He sensed her holding him at arm's length and couldn't figure out why. He knew when a woman found him attractive. But Marnie wasn't acting on her feelings, and the only reason that made sense was that she still had a thing for this Barry guy.

So Zach was really up for a Barry confrontation. "Marnie, you're still checking the door. Don't look so eager."

"Cool and sophisticated. Gotcha." She gave him a blasé look and sipped her beer. "I'm not just looking for Barry, you know. Lots of people from work come here. I'm hoping word will get back to Barry."

"Then we'd better look more like a happy couple."

"Oh? And how do we do that?"

If ever a man had an opening, this was it. But when Zach tried to analyze what women actually did to let him know they were interested, he blanked on specifics. "Touching," he said. Yeah, let Barry get a load of that.

"In public? I don't think so." Marnie popped a peanut into her mouth and added the shell to the growing pile next to her.

"Not that kind of touching." Zach stood up and slid

next to Marnie onto the brown leather bench under the stained-glass windows advertising various beers. He had been sitting in a chair across the table from her. "This kind." He draped an arm across her shoulders and drew her next to him so that their thighs were pressed together. He would have enjoyed it more if she'd been wearing a skirt, but she was wearing black pants.

"Oh, the this-is-my-property kind."

Zach felt an elbow close to his ribs. He leaned close enough to smell her shampoo. "Uncross your arms and relax." He tucked her hair behind her ear, enjoying the silkiness.

"What are you doing?"

"Grooming."

She uncrossed her arms at that, only to turn to him, mouth open. "*What?*"

"It's part of the courtship phase. Couples groom each other. You brush imaginary lint off my shirt, straighten my tie, that kind of thing."

"You're not wearing a tie."

"And you're not grooming."

She peered up at him. "There's nothing to groom."

"There doesn't have to be. The object is to touch, to create intimacy." And it worked. She'd forgotten all about the door and Zach had an excuse to get close to her. A winner all the way around.

"How do you know all this?"

Zach smoothed her hair over her shoulder. "The Internet is hardly your secret."

"Touching, huh?" She looked down. "Our legs are touching."

"I know." Did he ever know. He moved his fingers in lazy circles against her shoulder and she relaxed marginally.

"Touch me," he commanded softly, wondering if she heard the strain in his voice.

"Well, I don't..." Hesitantly, she smoothed a wrinkle on his sleeve.

"You should smile when you do that."

She bared her teeth.

"Marnie." Shaking his head, Zach picked up his beer mug.

Marnie exclaimed softly and reached for his hand. Zach gladly let go of the mug. "You hurt yourself."

He'd nicked a couple of knuckles earlier today when he'd been thinking about her instead of paying attention to what he was doing. "No big deal."

Marnie took a paper napkin, moistened it in the icy condensation on the side of her beer mug and then pressed it against his fingers. "Feel better?"

Zach smiled. She was a fast learner. "Very nicely done."

Marnie shot him an indignant look. "This isn't for show. You should probably have a bandage over those scrapes. You've got too many scars as it is."

"Kiss it and make it better," he suggested and braced himself for her protests. She'd probably slug him.

But Marnie pushed aside the napkin and pressed warm lips against his first knuckle. Heat shot straight to his groin. Her gentle kiss was completely the opposite of what he'd expected and caught him with his guard down. And his guard was still down when she looked up at him.

She was in his arms. She was soft and warm and pretty and she'd touched him. Was still touching him.

And not just physically. Marnie had gotten under his skin and into his heart. He thought about her constantly, though he tried not to. She was the sort of woman for whom a man shifted his priorities. And didn't mind doing it.

Right then, Zach admitted to himself that he couldn't let her go. How could he never see her again? How could he be satisfied with the few minutes they talked when she walked by the work site mornings and evenings? And after the job was finished, then what?

Didn't she want more, too?

They'd been looking at each other for long moments. The sound from the television over the bar faded away. The fact that they were in a sports bar became irrelevant.

Zach forgot about putting on a show for Barry. He forgot that Marnie considered him a coach. She was a woman he was falling for and he wanted to let her know it. Lowering his head, he drew her to face him.

He kissed her, kissed with a gentleness he didn't know he was capable of. An overwhelming tenderness swept over him taking him totally by surprise. When he'd thought about kissing Marnie again, gentle and tender weren't words he'd thought of. He'd thought he was pretty much in the desperately-hot-for-her camp.

But Marnie was different, he'd known that right

from the beginning. From the moment he first saw her on the balcony, he'd been drawn to her with an intensity that had never lessened. One minute she wasn't in his life and the next minute she was. He was going to keep her there and had no intention of playing fair.

Her lips were salty from the peanuts and Zach touched the edges with the tip of his tongue.

A tremor shuddered through Marnie and her lips turned soft and responsive. Zach gladly deepened the kiss, raising his free hand with the banged up knuckles to cup her face.

And then she was out of his arms, her hands pressed against his chest, her breath coming faster than normal.

Her eyes were wide, but her mouth—the same one he'd just been kissing—was set in an angry line. "What were you doing? Grooming my teeth?"

"Kissing you."

"Well…tone it down, okay?" She gripped her beer mug with both hands and looked appealingly flushed. "I'm not used to men who kiss the way you do."

"How do I kiss?"

Still gripping the mug, Marnie closed her eyes. "It's like your kisses are undiluted or something."

"So you liked kissing me." This was the best thing he'd heard all evening. He allowed himself a little internal gloating.

Marnie shot him a quick, resentful look.

Now was the time to tell her to ditch her plan for confronting what's-his-name and talk about this thing between them. Because, clearly she wasn't as immune to him as—

"Marnie?"

Marnie's head swiveled. "Doug?" She smiled widely. "Hey, how're you doing?"

"*Marnie?*" A tall, thin guy with bug eyes blinked at her. "I didn't recognize you."

"It has been a while since you've seen me. Eaten any good meatball subs lately?"

"Oh. Yeah." He turned a deep red visible even in the mottled light of the stained-glass windows.

Zach nudged her foot with his. Marnie glanced at him and he raised his eyebrows as he linked his little finger with one of hers.

"Zach, this is Doug from work. Doug, this is Zach."

Zach held out his free hand and shook Doug's. "Always glad to meet one of Marnie's friends. Join us?"

His little finger was getting squeezed. Zach squeezed back.

"Uh, okay." Doug looked dazed.

"There's plenty of room." Zach pried his finger away from Marnie, grimacing as the blood pounded back into it, and flung his arm around her. "Scoot over, babe." He pulled her next to him, enjoying himself.

Marnie made herself as stiff and as unyielding as a human body could get and still breathe.

Doug sat on the other side of her, ordered a beer and stared.

These brainiacs weren't much in the conversation department. Zach tried a little territorial grooming on Marnie and got a warning shot in the ribs with her elbow for his trouble.

"Y-you don't work at Carnahan," Doug finally managed to say after he got his beer.

"I'm in the construction business," Zach said.

"He restores Victorian houses," Marnie elaborated. And was that a hint of pride in her voice? Zach thought it might just be.

He dropped a kiss on the top of her head and clenched his stomach muscles. Surprisingly, Marnie didn't jab him, but he thought Doug's eyes would pop out.

"Uhm, look, uhm, I'm, uh..." He gulped some of the beer and stood, hooking a thumb over his shoulder. "I'm going to watch the game if you..." He trailed off.

"You go ahead. We're comfy here," Zach said and Doug escaped to the bar.

Marnie turned to Zach. "*Comfy?* Is that what we are?"

"Some of us more than others," Zach said. "You have a real problem with physical intimacy."

"Well, in a *bar,* yeah." She absently brushed a piece of peanut shell from his sleeve.

"Then we need to leave the bar." Zach drained his mug and slid off the bench, an inspired idea forming.

"Why?"

He held out his hand. "Because you need kissing lessons—unless you want them here."

"Ki—! Don't be ridiculous. There's nothing wrong with my kissing."

"If that's a sample of your best stuff, then you've got problems." Zach kept his voice and expression as detached as possible.

Slack-jawed, Marnie looked up at him. "I beg your

pardon! That was not my 'best stuff.' I don't go around doling out my 'best stuff' in bars."

"All the more reason to go back to your place." Zach gestured impatiently. "Come on. I've got to get an early start tomorrow. Besides, Dougie over there is going to spread the word about you and I'll bet your Barry will come by to see you for himself tomorrow. You'll want to be confident when you make your move, so it's now or never."

"You're kidding...aren't you?" She looked adorably uncertain.

They had to leave now, or he wouldn't be responsible for his actions. "I would never kid about something as serious as kissing."

Marnie slipped her hand into his and stood. "Nobody has ever complained about my kissing before."

Zach steered her toward the entrance. "Maybe they didn't know any better."

"And you do?"

As he opened the door, Zach grinned down at her. "Oh, yeah."

HOW COULD SHE shiver when her blood felt so hot?

Because she knew this wasn't a good idea, that's how. Hadn't she decided that Zach wasn't for her? She was opening herself up to hurt. Really, anyone could predict what would happen if they got together. At first, it would be great. They'd have a few hot days, maybe even weeks, but ultimately, he'd want to spend more and more time working, and she'd resent him for it, and he'd resent her for resenting and making him feel guilty, and she'd feel guilty that her resentment made him feel guilty for his resentment... It sounded confusing, but it was crystal clear to Marnie.

Her mind tried to protect her, but her body was jumping around in little circles demanding to know when the kissing lessons would start.

Not that she believed she needed them. At least she didn't *think* so. But she did have that element of doubt that should be eliminated. Besides, to Zach, it was only a few kisses. Look how matter-of-fact he was about it. She'd be matter-of-fact, too. Just watch her out matter-of-fact him.

"Zach is going to give me kissing lessons," Marnie announced matter-of-factly to Franco as they passed him on their way upstairs to the apartment.

Franco clutched at his heart. Marnie just hoped he wouldn't eavesdrop outside the door.

"Apparently, I am deficient when it comes to kissing," she said. "I don't have the *extensive* experience Zach does."

"It's quality, not quantity," Zach murmured.

He sounded almost bored. Couldn't he show a *little* enthusiasm?

How humiliating. Was her kissing that bad? She hadn't had a fair shot with Zach. Both times she hadn't been expecting to be kissed and wasn't sure she should be kissing him in the first place.

As opposed to now, when she had plenty of notice and *knew* she shouldn't be kissing him.

"*Mr.* Renfro." Franco had recovered from his heart palpitations.

"Somebody has to teach her," Zach called down the stairs.

"Marnie?"

"It's okay, Franco." Marnie unlocked her door.

So Zach felt he needed to improve her technique. She wondered if she was allowed to enjoy the lessons.

She wondered if he would.

Marnie flipped on the lights and threw her purse onto a chair. What now? Offer mouthwash?

"Wow," Zach said. He'd gone directly to the fireplace and was running his hands across the mantel. "I'd like to meet whoever did this work."

Any hope that Marnie had that Zach was using kissing lessons as an excuse for an extended makeout session vanished. She sighed. "Ask Franco. The apartment belongs to him. He rents it out and lives in the basement."

"How can he stand to? I mean, look—there're period furnishings."

"*Uncomfortable* period furnishings." Marnie indicated the rosewood Victorian leather settee with the typical hump in the middle. Where were these lessons going to take place? Were they supposed to kiss over the hump?

"If I owned this place, I'd never leave." He was staring at the crown molding.

Could her humiliation be any greater? Faced with kissing her, Zach chose to study the ceiling.

"Zach, are you going to kiss me, or not?"

Still looking at the ceiling, he answered, his voice gentle. "We don't have to do this if you don't want to."

That answered the greater humiliation question. "If *I* don't want to? I'm not the one staring at the ceiling!"

He inhaled so deeply, she saw his chest rise and fall. Then he turned and walked toward her. "I'm not the one standing in the center of the room, wringing my hands and turning red and white so fast the guy I'm with is thinking about calling 9-1-1."

Marnie felt her face flush. "You embarrassed me," she mumbled.

"You haven't been embarrassed about anything else so far." He came to a halt directly in front of her. Definitely in her personal space. "You're the woman who told me all about her sexual philosophy before we ordered dinner."

"That was different."

"Yes. We weren't alone." With his index finger, he tilted her chin up. "I'm going to kiss you now and I want you to relax. When you're ready, kiss me back."

At that moment, Marnie learned firsthand the definition of a Victorian swoon. Her heart started beating so hard she thought she was going to faint.

Oh, for pity's sake. It wasn't as though she'd never kissed anyone before. So this was Zach. So he was handsome. So he was appealing. So he was about to kiss her. So what?

These weren't real kisses. These were like stage kisses. For show.

Zach was looking at her, waiting patiently. If she were smart, she'd close her eyes and tilt her chin up.

If she were smart, she wouldn't have agreed to this, so why start now? She looked into his eyes.

Aw, nuts. His eyes held a mixture of amusement and banked desire. Desire for her. Desire from a man she never thought she could attract and knew she shouldn't anyway.

And so help her, she couldn't fight it any longer.

Oh, she knew this feeling. This was exactly like the time when she'd been talked into riding a new monster roller coaster with her dad. She hadn't wanted to, but she'd wanted to be with him. The whole time the cars chugged up to the top, she'd tried to convince herself it wouldn't be so bad and then there was that moment of suspension right at the top when she could see the downward fall and she knew the ride was going to be as scary as she thought. She'd wanted out. But it was too late.

She sighed and her eyes drifted shut.

Zach slowly leaned his head forward and very softly, he brushed his lips across hers. A jolt shot through her. At first she thought it might be static electricity, but realized it was Zach.

This preliminary convergence of lips wasn't quite a kiss and it left Marnie wanting more. She had never, ever wanted more of her last boyfriend's kisses. Not like this. She remembered thinking that if she just kept kissing him, she'd eventually feel something more than pleasantness. A zing. A zingette even. Zach had hardly touched her and already her chest felt tight and it was hard to breathe.

There was another featherlight touch at the corner of her mouth, then she felt Zach's lips against her cheek as he inhaled.

"Great shampoo," he whispered. "I bought six bottles at the drugstore trying to find out which one it was."

"It came from a salon," she murmured.

His breath made her shiver. Slowly moving back to her lips he gently touched them with his.

Marnie's heart was beating so hard, she knew he had to feel it. Her lips were exquisitely sensitive. She could feel the skin of his jaw, newly smooth from a recent shave. When she breathed in, she could smell his shaving cream.

Had she ever noticed a man's shaving cream? Had she ever taken the time to notice? There was something intimate in knowing that Zach used a woodsy-scented shaving cream. And that he'd bothered to shave before meeting her this evening.

The knowledge that he'd taken time to prepare for her warmed a place in her heart that had been long-neglected.

Marnie thought about the afternoon she'd spent getting ready to see Zach last week. The anticipation was part of the pleasure. That was the lesson he was teaching her now with this soft first meeting of their lips.

Zach drew back and looked into her unfocused eyes, then finally, finally, he dipped his head and kissed her. Lightly at first, then with more pressure and at last a full kiss. His hand caressed her cheek before he slid it into her hair, cupping the back of her head and drawing her closer.

Okay, so she was in the hands—and lips—of a master. She knew nothing.

But she was ready to learn.

Zach teased her lips, lightly taking her lower one between his and sucking gently. Marnie gripped his arms just to keep her balance, but even if her knees gave out—a distinct possibility—she knew she wouldn't fall as long as Zach held her.

At this point, most guys' tongues would be in her mouth, but Zach concentrated on her lips. It felt so good that Marnie barely noticed that his thumb was massaging her nape and his other hand was nestled in the small of her back moving in warming circles.

She leaned into his kiss drawing her arms around him. He felt so good and solid and safe, though she wasn't aware of feeling unsafe before. He nibbled and nipped and savored and sampled.

And Marnie enjoyed every moment of it.

She sensed that the kiss was about to end before it did because Zach gradually lightened the pressure, echoing the beginning of the kiss, but in reverse. A coda.

Marnie sighed when it was over and he dropped his hands. "Wow." She didn't let go of him because she knew she'd stagger if she tried to walk. "That was...that was...pretty good."

"Why didn't you kiss me back?" he asked gravely.

Hadn't she? No, she'd lost herself in the moment—in several moments. "I forgot," she said.

Zach bent his head until his forehead was touching hers. "Kiss me now."

She could do this. She could enjoy kissing him and walk away afterward. Clearly she had a lot to learn and this was good for her. Experiencing some first-class kissing would keep her from settling for less. This was a good thing.

Marnie raised herself on tiptoes and they bumped noses. "I'm hopeless!" she moaned.

"Marnie?" Zach leaned down.

"What?"

"Shut. Up. And. Kiss. Me."

Well, when he put it *that* way.... Marnie locked her lips on his. Okay, she skipped some of the gentle stuff. So sue her.

She improvised a little nibbling, then took Zach's upper lip in her mouth and pulled on it. There was an answering tug on her lower lip that she felt deep within her. Zach was kissing her, too. Mental note: dual participation makes kissing much better.

And she hadn't thought it could be better. She parted her lips, inviting him to do the same, but instead, Zach trailed a string of kisses along her jaw to her ear and the sensitive area right behind it.

Marnie dropped her head back, but when she caught herself about to moan, she dragged Zach's mouth back to hers. No revealing that she was wildly turned on. This was a demo only.

Still, she buried her fingers in his hair and pressed her body to his, wanting more and knowing she couldn't have it.

Zach covered her hands with his and pulled them away. "Oooookay." He blinked and drew a deep breath. "Good job."

"Thanks." She didn't know what else to say.

"You see how exploring another person's skin texture, taste and scent can be...pleasant?"

"Very pleasant," Marnie agreed.

"Remember not to rush that kind of kissing. Too

many people do and they miss out." He gave her a half smile. "Too many guys want to skip ahead. You should insist that they take their time."

"Oh, I will. Insist on it." Marnie nodded her head vigorously. "At the very next opportunity."

"And you have to kiss back."

"I know. I was—I was learning."

"You learn very well."

"Thank you." So the conversation wasn't brilliant. Marnie was amazed that she could talk at all.

"Okay." Zach rolled back his shoulders and stretched his neck from side to side as though getting the kinks out. "Next up, French kissing."

Marnie's insides turned to liquid. "We'd better sit down." She looked doubtfully over at the settee, but Zach was already headed over there.

He sat down and patted the area beside him as casually as though they were getting ready to discuss blueprints or something.

Marnie wobbled her way across the room, hoping that Zach would mistake it for a sexy walk.

Be calm. Be cool. Be sophisticated. She sat and the cushion squeaked.

Zach maneuvered her closer. "There are a couple of tricks to this—"

"I knew there would be."

"Nothing complicated. When I'm kissing a woman, I always appreciate a signal that she's ready to take the kiss to the next level."

Marnie thought she'd signaled pretty clearly during the last kiss. "The fact that she's melted into a little puddle at your feet isn't signal enough?"

"Not when I'm having a meltdown of my own."

Marnie tried to envision Zach having a meltdown, losing control because he desired a woman that much...desired her that much.

"If I don't get that signal," he continued. "I might run the tip of my tongue along the inner edge of her lip."

Marnie parted her lips as she imagined him doing so. "Then what?"

His gaze dropped to her mouth. "If you are so inclined, you part your lips just the way they are now. And feel free to take the initiative by doing the same to the man."

"Okay. What then?"

"Come here and I'll show you."

Marnie's heart hadn't recovered from the last demonstration. But she was game. Boy, was she game. She leaned toward him.

Apparently not fast enough. Zach more than met her halfway. One hand splayed across her back before the other adjusted the tilt of her head and he swooped in, starting this kiss where the last one had left off.

There was no argument from Marnie. She believed they'd pretty much mastered the art of the slow, seductive kiss.

You have to kiss back.

Right. Marnie looped her arms around Zach's neck and cupped his head. Then, just to show him that she'd been paying attention, Marnie ran the tip of her tongue across the seam of his lips.

She felt him smile.

"Nice," he murmured. "Open your mouth just a little. We aren't going *speelunking* here." He traced the outline of her lips with his tongue.

Marnie barely suppressed a whimper.

"There are all sorts of things you can do at this point," Zach murmured against her mouth.

"As long as it doesn't involve going for the tonsils or cutting off air supply."

He chuckled. "Poor Marnie." And promptly showed her a brand-new erogenous zone by curling his tongue and caressing the backside of her upper lip.

She gasped.

"I like that, too," he prompted, though he didn't need to because Marnie was already responding in kind.

And kept responding. He would gently pull her tongue into his mouth and she would pull back. She matched him stroke for stroke, plunge for plunge and duel for duel. They caressed, explored and circled.

"Don't forget about your hands," Zach instructed her at one point.

Naturally, she had. She began concentrating on the feel of his hair against her fingers and the muscles in his neck and jaw. Adding all that to the kiss put Marnie on sensory overload.

Yet she wanted more. She shifted and brought her hands between them, unbuttoning a couple of buttons on his shirt and slipping her fingers inside to smooth against the warm skin of his chest.

He inhaled sharply and leaned back. "Whoa. You're headed past kissing territory there."

Marnie was a little dizzy from the abrupt end to the

greatest kiss she'd ever had in her life. "You said use my hands."

"But they shouldn't unbutton, unbuckle, unhook or unsnap unless you're planning on getting naked, understand?"

Marnie was thinking that wasn't such a bad idea, but Zach wasn't encouraging her, so she played casual.

"Gotcha." She smiled, then pressed her fingers to her mouth. "My lips are numb!"

Grinning, Zach buttoned his shirt. "Then my work here is done."

Work. The lesson. What a mood killer. Marnie was still dazed and everything in her body that could throb was throbbing and Zach could just walk away.

Fine. So could she. As soon as her legs would work. "Great lesson, Zach. So how did I do?" Her voice sounded almost normal.

"You passed."

"Well, that's a relief. And I do want to thank you. I like the slow start. It really sensitizes the lips—at least until they go numb—and builds anticipation. Also, you become familiar with your partner's taste and scent. Nice technique."

He eyed her oddly. "I've always thought so."

"You've got some great tongue moves, too. The under-the-lip thing was a good one. I'll bet you've had good results with that one."

He rubbed a finger against his temple. "Are you asking for details?"

"No! No, oh, no. It was just a comment. And in that vein, I want to add how refreshing it was not to have a tongue jammed down my throat, or feel like I've been through a car wash, or worry about catching a breath between thrusts, or—"

"I don't need details, either, Marnie."

She wanted to forget those details anyway. Marnie cautiously put weight on her feet before attempting to stand. Zach stood, too. Smoothing her hair back, she led the way to her door. "Good night, Zach, and thanks again. I promise to put my newly learned techniques to good use."

ZACH DIDN'T WALK through the door. In fact, he closed the door. "You're talking about Barry, aren't you?"

"For now."

How could she say that? How could she stand there with her mouth rosy from his kisses and say that? He'd put his heart and soul and tongue into those kisses. And she'd...she'd dissected them.

She had to have felt something. She'd started unbuttoning his shirt. If that wasn't proof that she felt something, then he didn't know what the hell was.

Maybe he didn't know. Maybe he should have let her unbutton his shirt so he could find out. He couldn't believe that after those soul-fusing kisses she wanted to go out and practice her "techniques" on somebody else. On Barry.

"Forget about Barry." He grabbed her arm and led her back to the settee. On the way, he unbuttoned his shirt.

"Zach? What are you doing?"

"Going back in time."

When he got to the settee, he positioned her on it and sat next to her.

"Marnie—"

"This isn't a good idea." She jumped up.

Zach captured her hand and placed it against his chest. Marnie closed her eyes.

"Feel my heart beating?"

"Damn it, Zach!" She sank next to him and held her head with her other hand.

"Forget Barry," he urged her. "You know there's something between us."

"I'm...I'm not your type."

"You are now."

"I don't go around looking like this all the time."

"You look fine."

"I'm..." Her voice dropped to a whisper. "I'm afraid of being hurt."

"Oh, Marnie." He sighed her name as a rush of feeling coursed through him. "I could never hurt you." He didn't know what else he could say or how he could prove it to her.

Beneath his hand her fingers slowly clenched and unclenched.

Zach released his hold on her. Marnie stared at her hand on his chest. Catching her lower lip between her teeth, she spread her fingers, then brought her other hand up, too.

Zach knew she could feel his heart pounding like a jackhammer and he was glad. He forced himself not to move, letting her take the lead, letting her learn to trust him.

Marnie dreamily drew her fingers over his skin

moving across his chest, up over his shoulders and pushing his shirt down his arms. Then she bent her head and kissed him on his chest, right above his heart.

"Marnie." He barely recognized the sandpapery rasp of his voice. With a hand on either side of her head, he brought her lips to his. He wanted her. Now. And that's the way he kissed her—with all the passion that he'd held back before. He actually shook with the intensity of his feelings. It was incredible. He felt both powerful and powerless at the same time. No woman had ever made him feel this way.

He knew these emotions were very new and had developed very fast. But it was always the houses that went together quickly that were the most solidly built—everything fit perfectly the first time. Why wouldn't relationships be the same way?

If Marnie felt even half of what he was feeling, he could understand her doubt, her hesitation.

That didn't mean he didn't try to convince her to see things his way. Maybe it wasn't fair—no, definitely not fair—but Zach began building a sensual world for the two of them. He murmured soothing words against her ear as he enfolded her in his arms and stroked her hair. He nibbled tiny kisses on her temple, cheeks and the corner of her mouth.

With a sigh that sounded as though it originated from the depths of her being, Marnie nestled her cheek against his shoulder and ran her hands inside his shirt. Zach dropped a kiss on the top of her head and held her close.

"Zach..." Marnie murmured softly and was utterly still.

Then she exhaled with a soft moan. Zach felt all the tension leave her body and knew it was the moment she'd decided to stop fighting her feelings.

That and the fact that she turned in his arms and straddled him, then tugged his shirt out of the waistband of his jeans. She planted frantic kisses over his face and mouth as she pulled his shirt off his arms and dropped it beside her.

"You're such a man, Zach." Her gaze admiring, Marnie ran her hands over his chest and squeezed his shoulders as she spoke. Lowering her mouth to his, she groaned as she slid her hands to his back. "I love the feel of your skin," she said against his mouth.

Yes. Skin. Skin was good.

Marnie had skin, too. Skin Zach desperately wanted to touch. Soft skin. Warm skin. Hidden skin.

His fingers had found the edge of her sweater and burrowed beneath it when Marnie abruptly broke the kiss and twisted away.

"I can't do this," she whispered, her knuckles to her mouth.

Zach could barely speak. "Too fast?" He was crazy with want. For him it wasn't fast enough.

She shook her head but stood and smoothed her sweater. She wouldn't meet his eyes. "Too everything. You're a wonderful man, but you told me yourself that your work means everything to you. I admire and respect that, but I can't get involved with someone who won't put me and our relationship first. We're at different places in our lives, that's all."

Too many words, but their meaning was clear. Zach dragged air into his lungs. "That's it? You're going to throw away something this special without giving me a chance?" He was so stunned he could barely speak.

Now she did look at him and her eyes glistened with unshed tears. "I can't afford to give you a chance."

"Marnie—"

"Please leave."

Fine. He'd leave. For now. Only for now. He stood, grabbed his shirt and buttoned it as he headed to the door and yanked it open. "Just tell me—is it because of Barry?"

"No."

"Are you still planning to go out with him?"

Marnie tilted her chin up. "If he asks me to Tarantella."

Breathing hard, Zach stared at her in disbelief. "Have fun," he said quietly and closed the door.

Once in the hallway, he wanted to bang his head against the wall. What just happened? Why? She'd rejected him, but not because of Barry? Sure. Right.

Zach understood too fast. He understood "not now."

He did not understand "not ever," unless another guy was involved.

When Zach reached the bottom of the stairs, a voice accosted him out of the dark foyer.

"I assume Marnie is all right?" Franco, standing guard.

"Marnie is just fine. More than fine. Great. Maybe even more than great."

"And you?" came the surprising question.

"I'll be okay," Zach muttered. "I'd never hurt her, you know. No matter what she thinks."

"I know. Had I believed otherwise, I wouldn't have allowed you up the stairs."

Zach was already at the front door, but he circled back, located Franco sitting by the telephone table in the gloom and stuck out his hand. "You're okay, Frank."

Franco shook his outstretched hand. "I aspire to much more than 'okay,' but thank you."

9

I AM OKAY. Apparently very high praise. I do like Mr. Renfro even though we are not simpatico. He and M. are very simpatico, though they are in deep denial. Bad for them, but good for me as people in deep denial behave in intriguingly illogical ways.

MARNIE WAS LATE to work because she'd overslept because she hadn't been able to get to sleep because she'd been kissed senseless by Zach. And just because.

She wore her new coat, her black slacks and her turquoise sweater set and, though she was tempted to tie it back, she left her hair loose and flicked the mascara brush at her eyes and swiped lipstick on her mouth. And then she had to put concealer around her mouth because it was faintly red from her extended kissing session with Zach.

She didn't have time for either breakfast or coffee and certainly not for walking the long way around the office in hopes of seeing Barry. She didn't want to deal with Barry today.

Naturally he was waiting for her by her cubicle. He let out a wolf whistle. Finally. Too bad it was from Barry.

"Hi, Barry." She swept past him and hung up her coat.

"Marnie?"

Barry lacked finesse. Marnie hadn't been quite so aware of it before. He should have given her an approving once-over and said something like, "Lookin' good, kid."

"What did you do to yourself?" he asked.

"Not much. I got my hair cut."

"But you look so different!"

This guy was just full of charm. What had she ever seen in him? He leaned against her cubicle wall, still with the unflattering expression on his face.

But Marnie shook it off. "I rented an apartment in town a couple of days a week and I have more time to get ready in the mornings."

She saw Barry's gaze drop to her mouth and wondered if the concealer had worn off. Turning away, she flipped on her computer and listened to the whirring and cracking it made as it booted up.

Now that she was alone with Barry, Marnie couldn't remember any of Zach's instructions. Conversation. She should ask a question since Barry wasn't saying anything on his own. "Haven't seen you around much lately." No, it wasn't a question, but it was a start.

"Yeah. I was at that business tech conference in Anaheim for a couple of days last week."

Marnie kept waiting for Barry to tell her she looked good. He obviously thought so. Or maybe it wasn't so obvious. Maybe she'd been a little to quick with the mascara this morning. Still, here he was and if she was going to make a move, now was the time. She flipped her hair over her shoulder and smoothed her sweater. Barry's eyes followed the movements of her hands.

He still looked stunned. Marnie was getting irritated with him.

"Are you and that guy Doug saw you with dating?"

"We've been out a couple of times." Finally remembering Zach's grooming talk, Marnie reached out and straightened Barry's collar. "I'm doing a Web site for him."

"He's a Carnahan client?" Barry frowned. Maybe he didn't know about grooming.

"I'm freelancing."

"Oh." He looked down at his feet. "Look, Marnie, about the other night."

"What about it?" Marnie scented victory. She inhaled deeply, even though it attracted Barry's attention to her breasts. And she wasn't even wearing the water balloon pads.

"I wanted to thank you for working on the animation module."

"You're welcome."

"And that other stuff—I was just giving you a hard time."

As much as she wanted to, Marnie couldn't claim victory from that. She tried more hair flicking and licked her lips.

Ick. She got a taste of concealer.

"Hey, you wanna go catch a movie?"

Marnie had no intention of dating up to a dinner at Tarantella. It was now or never. "Maybe dinner first?"

"Uh—yeah. We could stop off for a sandwich some place."

"A sandwich!" Marnie giggled and swore she never would again. "You're so funny! The first time we go out should be special." She licked her lips again and stepped close enough so she could look up at him through her eyelashes. "I haven't been out in such a looonnnggg time." *Come on, Barry.* "I'm in an *Italian* mood."

Barry's eyes glazed over. "You'd probably like Tarantella."

"I'd *love* Tarantella."

He swallowed. "Let's go there. T-tonight."

Finally. Getting the invitation was such work that Marnie almost turned him down. But at this point, he *owed* her a Tarantella dinner. "Great. Pick me up at...let's say seven-thirty?"

Barry nodded dumbly.

"Here's the address." Marnie took one of her business cards from the engraved brass holder on her desk and wrote out the apartment's address on the back. "Don't forget to make reservations," she said as she handed it to him.

"Okay. Sure." He blinked down at the address. "I'll be there."

Marnie smiled and slipped onto the chair in front of her computer. "I'll see you then." She waggled her fingers and put on her headphones.

Then she typed a reminder note into the calendar program so she'd remember to check and see if Barry actually made the reservations.

MARNIE LEFT exactly on time so she would be sure to catch Zach. But since he always worked until dusk anyway, she wasn't too worried. There would be an initial awkwardness, but she wanted him to know that she appreciated his help and that she'd finally wangled her Tarantella invitation.

When she reached the corner, Marnie stopped, got into attractive-female mode and threw back her shoulders. She strolled around the corner, ready to accept the whistles of the workers. She was willing them to notice her, so at first, she didn't realize what they were doing. A sign was planted in the front yard, and Marnie nodded to herself, thinking that it was about time Zach got a sign advertising his work. But then she saw two men hammering a four-by-eight piece of plywood over one of the downstairs windows. All the windows were covered in plywood. Thinking it was odd, Marnie entered the yard and stared at the sign.

It read For Sale.

That couldn't be good. Ignoring the fact that the construction workers had barely noticed her, let alone whistled at her, Marnie called to them in between shots from the nail gun, "Is Zach inside?"

Both nodded, so Marnie picked her way around sheets of stacked plywood and went inside the house. "Zach?"

There was no answer. She peered up the stairs, but since they'd been stripped, she wasn't about to climb them. Maybe if she were wearing her old hiking boots, but she wasn't. She headed toward what was once the kitchen, then through the dining room. "Zach?"

"Marnie?" He was in the living room by the fireplace, his fingers tracing one blue-and-white Delft tile.

When she saw him, all awkwardness fled. "Zach, what happened?"

He looked awful, as though someone had died. Actually, for him, that wasn't far off. "The owners pulled the plug."

"I'm sorry."

"Yeah." His voice was gruff. He was in mourning.

"It was the ugly wallpaper, wasn't it?" Marnie tried to lighten his mood. "They just couldn't face having it in this room."

Zach managed a weak smile. "No. It was a divorce."

"But you only started here a few weeks ago."

"They hired me a year ago."

"You book a *year* in advance?"

"Sometimes more." He ran his hand through his hair. "What can I say? I'm good."

"You're slow."

Shooting her a look, he said, "I only work for people who want the job done right."

"So now this job doesn't get done at all."

His jaw hardened. "Maybe. Depends on who buys the house, whether they restore or raze and start over."

Marnie could just imagine what happened. The strain of waiting for their dream house was too much for a couple who were living in crowded temporary quarters while Zach indulged in perfectionism.

Sometimes his perfectionism was good, fabulous even, such as when applied to kissing. Marnie allowed herself a sigh as she imagined what else he'd perfected—and it had nothing to do with Victorian houses.

"At any rate," he patted the fireplace as though comforting it. "Somebody will get a real bargain."

"Why don't *you* buy it?" Marnie asked.

"We've been through this. I don't have the cash for the down payment."

"That's why you need to change the way you work."

Glaring at her, he snapped, "No—I—do—not!" Each word was delivered with the punch of a nail gun.

"But Zach, you've mentioned how it's your dream to own a Painted Lady and fix it the way you want. Yet the way you run your business isn't helping you accomplish your goal. You don't charge enough. You do everything yourself and take forever doing it. You barely make enough to support yourself and when it's all over, somebody else gets to live in the houses and you go back to an apartment that apparently is so scummy, you didn't want me to see it."

"Leave it, Marnie."

She shook her head. "You are so stubborn."

"I thought you'd understand, but you're just like every other woman I've ever met!"

He meant it as an insult, but to Marnie it was a compliment. "I understand, but I don't happen to agree with you. There's a difference."

"The bottom line is the same."

There was no sense reasoning with him until he'd had a chance to cool down. "I am sorry about this,

Zach. Anyway, I stopped by to tell you that I'm going out with Barry to Tarantella tonight."

He nodded slowly. "Congratulations. I know it's what you wanted."

They locked gazes, then glanced away.

"Thank you for...everything."

"You're welcome for...everything."

"Wish me luck?"

"You'll be fine."

"FRANCO, MAY I please borrow the skirt? I've tried to find one like it, but I can't." Marnie had tried on her sparkly top with the slacks, but it didn't look right.

Franco was on hold with the cable company as he sorted the day's mail. "I'm not surprised." He held up one finger and spoke into the phone. "No, the cable man did not come today. You promised between twelve and four. It is now six-thirty. Uh-huh. Uh-huh. Thursday morning between eight and twelve. Please note that Mrs. Gilroy is paying someone to be available to admit your man and should he not arrive between eight and twelve on Thursday morning, you will receive a bill." Franco hung up the phone. "Half a day lost. At least I was able to work on my script. Now, tell me what's going on."

"I'm going to dinner at Tarantella with Barry tonight."

"Why?"

"You remember...Barry?"

"Yes, I remember. Dinner with Barry...what an interesting choice." He looked off into the distance. Actually, he looked in the direction of Zach's house.

Marnie uncomfortably noted that he did *not* write in his notebook. Not a good sign. "May I borrow the skirt?"

"What are you wearing with it?"

Marnie had brought the sparkly top to show him because she knew he'd ask. She held it up.

Franco winced.

"Bronze is one of my colors! And it's got sparkles."

"Were there any sparkles on your swatches?"

"No."

"There were no sparkles for a reason."

"Well, *I* like it," Marnie told him defiantly. In truth, she still felt it might be too much, but she was in that kind of mood tonight.

Franco sighed. "You can take the girl out of the suburbs, but you can't take the suburbs out of the girl. Go. Take the skirt—it's in the basement closet and—"

"Report back, I know, I know."

ZACH WAS *not* fine. First his current job was down the tubes and now this. Marnie was really going out with slimeball Barry. How could she? Yeah, he knew that's what she wanted, but that was before last night. How could she ignore last night? *He* couldn't ignore last night. Yeah, he'd heard what she said, but had he ever put work ahead of her?

This evening hadn't helped his cause. He'd been angry with both the clients and himself for blowing the job and he'd taken it out on her. Though she hadn't acted hurt or angry and in fact, had acted way more maturely than he had, she was *still* going out with a guy who'd treated her like garbage.

Zach was carrying tools out to his Bronco when he saw a car double park in front of the pink-and-green Victorian. A man wearing a white shirt and a slight paunch got out. Barry?

Zach waited and several moments later, the guy came down the steps with Marnie.

Marnie. He felt as though he'd been sucker punched. At first glance, it looked like she wasn't wearing anything from the waist up. She was, but her shoulders were bare and she was wearing a skirt and some sexy little shoes. Barry put his hand across her back to help her into the car and Zach's field of vision narrowed.

The guy had his hands on Marnie. Zach's Marnie. And Marnie had said she was going to practice her newly learned kissing techniques on this Barry sleaze.

No way.

Forgetting the rest of his tools, Zach got into the Bronco and followed the car as it pulled away from the curb.

EVEN FOR CASUAL, Zach was severely underdressed for Tarantella. He ducked into the men's room and threw water on his face, slicked back his hair, then went to see about getting a table.

"Do you have a reservation?" asked the sweet young thing manning the hostess station.

"No, but I tip heavy." Zach put a twenty on top of the book. "I tip more if I don't have to wait."

The twenty disappeared. "Um. Just a minute."

While Zach considered whether that constituted waiting, the girl slipped off the stool and went to a coatrack. Pulling off a sports jacket, she slipped it over his shoulders. "Just so you'll be more comfortable," she said.

The sleeves were too short and the jacket wouldn't button. How was he supposed to be comfortable?

On the other hand, he thought as he followed the girl to a table, did he expect to be comfortable while Marnie was trying to seduce another man?

He saw them at once, brazenly sitting in the center of the half-empty room. Yes, half-empty. Either everyone ate late, or he'd just wasted twenty dollars. Marnie had her back to him, so Zach had a chance to check out Barry when he passed by.

He had a scraggly-looking yuppie goatee thing going and a pasty complexion. This was the competition?

Zach felt better.

But not much.

The hostess tried to lead him to the very back where single diners were apparently banished, but Zach took a seat at a table against the wall not too far from where Marnie and Barry were seated. He figured his twenty ought to buy him location at least.

Without a word, the girl returned and handed him a menu. Zach thanked her and when he looked over at his quarry, he saw Marnie looking right at him, her eyes wide with surprise. Or maybe anger. But not lust. Definitely not lust. But that could change.

He held her gaze, then blew her a kiss. She rolled her eyes, then turned her attention to Barry. Her complete attention. She might have been making a training video for seduction.

Zach had to sit there and watch as she flirted and leaned and *groomed* and generally bedazzled the guy with everything he'd taught her. Come to think of it, Marnie had taken to everything quite naturally, even embellishing, so how much had he really taught her?

Marnie leaned forward and touched Barry's hand and laughed. And what, Zach wanted to know, was so damn funny about that?

Then her salad arrived and she picked a cherry tomato out of it and offered it to Barry, playfully feeding it to him and letting her fingers linger against his mouth.

Zach was very sure he hadn't taught her anything like that. Not that it wasn't a good ploy.

Marnie looked great tonight. Make that hot and great. Incandescent. The restaurant wasn't crowded, but she'd been the recipient of covert looks. Her arms and shoulders gleamed in the light, her smile bewitched and tantalized. Zach wanted to blindfold everybody.

So, what was the point of this dinner? From what Zach could overhear, Barry was too overwhelmed by Marnie to carry on much of a conversation.

Zach barely ate his dinner—some chicken thing—but they finished theirs and the bill arrived. Barry glanced over it as Marnie sipped her water. He leaned forward and said something to her. At that moment Marnie, who had studiously been avoiding eye contact with Zach, flicked her gaze in his direction. Some of the brightness left her face as she stared back at Barry. One brow arched upward.

Barry turned the bill toward her. Zach's jaw

dropped as Marnie reached for her purse. *No. The man always pays.* He distinctly remembered telling her that.

She got out her wallet and Zach nearly marched over there and collared the guy. Instead, he willed her to look his way, but she wouldn't. They got up and left.

Zach could see Marnie's shoulder blades. Everyone could see Marnie's shoulder blades. Barry put his hand over Marnie's shoulder blades.

Zach should be putting his hand over Marnie's shoulder blades. Touching her smooth skin…turning her to face him. Taking her mouth with his…

If he hadn't been blindsided by sudden lust, he would have remembered that he didn't know where they were going.

He threw down several bills and headed after them.

"Sir?" The hostess stopped him.

"What?" Zach strained to see which way Marnie and Barry went.

"The jacket?"

Zach shed the jacket and made it to the parking lot as they pulled out. He eventually caught up with them, easing back when he realized they were headed for Marnie's apartment.

Maybe the guy would just drop her off. Zach parked in his old spot in the yard of the house he'd been restoring. Marnie and the guy went inside the building.

Zach sat in his truck counting off the minutes until Barry returned. Barry didn't return. When Zach couldn't stand it anymore, he slammed the door of the Bronco and marched across the street.

BARRY WAS *B-O-R-I-N-G.* How could she have ever been the slightest bit interested in him?

Barry was telling her boring stories about his boring life and discussing boring problems with his boring job and never once asked her anything. Before, he at least talked shop with her, but now he was acting as though she had no brains.

Marnie had given him a tour of the apartment minus the bedroom, during which the skirt Franco had lent her had turned scratchy and stuck to her legs. Now they were standing back in the living room and Marnie was trying to decide if she should offer coffee or encourage him to sit on the leather settee.

The same leather settee where she'd indulged in prime quality kissing with Zach.

Maybe not the settee. However, it might not make any difference. She'd flirted, touched Barry so much she'd practically pawed him, and still he hadn't made a move toward her. She'd now decided that if he ever moved in for a kiss, she'd pull back and say, "I guess this means you find me attractive, maybe even girlfriend material?" He'd nod and she'd say, "That's all I wanted to know" and throw him out.

It was a pretty good script, she thought, one Franco would approve. Only somebody forgot to tell Zach that there wasn't a part in the script for him.

There was a knock on the door. "Maintenance."

Marnie immediately recognized Zach's voice. She wasn't even surprised after he'd stalked them at the restaurant, the reason for which she fully intended to take up with him later. But not now.

Barry looked at his watch. "They're racking up the overtime tonight."

"Seems that way." Marnie smiled at him. "Would you like some...coffee?"

"Aren't you going to open the door?"

"I think he's knocking at the apartment next door."

There came an unmistakable pounding on her door. The paintings on the wall moved. "Maintenance. We've had a report of a gas leak."

Clearly, Zach wasn't going away. Might as well get this over with. Stomping over to the door, she yanked it open. "Everything is fine in here."

"But you can't be sure." Zach hefted the tool belt he wore. "Gas is odorless and colorless."

"Which is why they put an odorant in it." Marnie tried to close the door, but he actually put his foot across the threshold. "And I suppose those are OSHA-approved steel-toed boots, right?" The door would break before his boots would.

"Absolutely," Zach said, bullying his way inside.

What did he think he was doing?

Zach gave Barry a dismissing once-over and asked her, "Where's your hot-water heater?"

Marnie had a choice. She could play along or she could reveal Zach's identity. He stared at her, challenging her to do precisely that.

So, naturally, she didn't. "I have no idea," Marnie said. "Don't you have a meter thingie that detects gas?"

"Not on me."

"Maybe you should schedule this...inspection for another time when you have your meter with you."

Zach rattled his tool belt. "I would never forgive myself if something happened to you in the meantime."

"Hey, Marnie, it's okay." Barry moved toward the door. "I've got to be getting home anyway."

With a furious look at Zach, Marnie walked Barry to the door hoping for a good-night kiss in front of Zach—wouldn't that be great?—or having him ask her to go out again or even offering a it's-been-great-and-man-have-you-changed comment. What she got was "See you tomorrow."

Marnie closed the door with deceptive gentleness before rounding on Zach. "What do you think you're doing?"

Zach took off his tool belt. "What do you think *you're* doing?"

"What I always said I would do—try to get Barry to admit that he was wrong about me, then tell him what a jerk he is." Marnie kicked off her oh-so-cute shoes with more force than necessary. They landed near Zach's stupid tool belt.

"He went to Tarantella with you—isn't that enough?"

"No."

"Yeah, I kinda noticed that you had to pay for your own dinner."

That was a sore point. "Barry was short on cash. I didn't give him enough notice today."

"Two words—credit card."

"I *know,*" she admitted. "Which is why I wanted to make my point a *little* more forcefully. Now I might have to go out with him again."

"Why?" Zach asked.

Couldn't he get it? "Because I want Barry drooling all over me, that's why! You weren't there that night. He was so...he was almost surprised that I'd even *consider* myself attractive to men. It was clear that he hadn't ever thought of me as a woman. I know we're all supposed to have evolved past this, but the thing is, if you're a female in our society, no matter what else you've accomplished, you're judged on your appearance and your appeal. So I want, *need* Barry to validate my attractiveness as a woman."

"What are you, a parking ticket? Barry can keep his drool to himself and if all you want is validation that you're a desirable woman, I can damn well take care of that." Zach stepped forward, grabbed her arms and hauled her toward him in a very me-man-you-woman way. Very effective move.

Dispensing with anything remotely resembling slow, gentle tenderness, Zach kissed her. It was passion all the way and it was just want Marnie needed at that moment.

She even remembered to kiss him back before he broke the kiss as forcefully as it had begun.

"Well?" He gazed down at her, all manly jaw and hot gaze.

Yes. Well. Marnie reassessed her situation. Against all odds, she'd attracted a hunky construction guy who was a very good kisser and probably an even better lover who currently had her in his arms and would, if he received the go-ahead, make mad, passionate love to her.

On the other hand, there was a ninety-eight percent

chance that she was going to get hurt. But if Zach walked out the door right now, she'd be hurt for sure.

A two-percent chance of happiness was looking better and better.

Zach's grip on her arms had loosened. "All I'm asking is for you to give us a chance."

She smiled whimsically. "A two-percent chance?"

"Whatever I can get."

"You know..." She ran her finger across his jaw. "I'm thinking you can get quite a lot."

"What do you mean?" Zach snarled, still in manly mode. With any luck, he'd stay that way.

"Validate me."

Zach's brows lowered. "You can't depend on someone else to—"

Marnie stopped him by putting her fingers against his mouth. "That was in reference to the parking ticket crack. How about this—kiss me, you fool?"

"You think I'm a fool?"

"If you don't kiss me you are."

ZACH WAS NO FOOL.

He was no fool, but he'd been holding back for so long with her that he simply couldn't any longer. Last night had been sweet torture ending in frustration when she wouldn't give him a chance to show her how important she was to him.

That's what bothered him the most. Marnie kept throwing around the term "girlfriend material," but she hadn't considered him "boyfriend material." She valued some jerk of a co-worker's opinion over Zach's.

But the co-worker wasn't here and Zach was. If he couldn't work with that, then he didn't deserve her.

"You're beautiful." He stared into her eyes so she could see how she affected him. "You're an incredibly desirable woman. Too much woman for Barry."

"Who?"

"Exactly." He smiled and drew his hands up and down her arms, touching the skin that he'd longed to feel earlier. Soft. So very soft. "In the restaurant...when he touched you...I wanted to drag him off you and pulverize him." He traced his fingers along her collarbone. "It was a visceral reaction. I wanted to commit violence in order to claim you."

Marnie gazed at him, unblinking.

"I wanted you." He smiled as his finger hooked one tiny strap and sent it slithering down her shoulder. "I still want you." Zach pressed his mouth to the spot on her shoulder where the strap had been and sucked gently.

Marnie shuddered and dropped her head back, exposing her neck. Zach took full advantage, though the blood pounded through his veins with such force he felt it in his eyes and ears. When he placed his mouth against her neck, he felt her pulse thundering, too.

He didn't want to frighten her—or himself. He controlled his movements with all the precision he devoted to working the powerful jigsaw—one slip and all would be lost.

"Zach," she whispered and turned her mouth to capture his.

Zach kissed her lightly but she pulled him back with an imperious "More!"

With that one word, everything changed. Zach kissed her again, parting her lips and pretty much ignoring all the careful techniques he'd taught her. He was going with raw feeling.

His tongue plunged into her mouth and he felt the vibrations of a moan and...was that her tonsil?

He pulled back, intending to apologize, when Marnie grabbed his face with both hands and plunged her tongue into *his* mouth, so he figured straying into tonsil territory wasn't an unpardonable sin.

He liked the way she held his face and took control of the kiss. He liked the way she drew herself closer and stood on her toes so her body curved into his. He liked everything at this point.

He ran his hands down her back and over her hips, sliding against the warm material of her skirt.

The fabric reminded him of the chocolate candy bar he'd accidentally left on his dashboard in the sun. He'd been hungry, so he'd eaten it anyway, and the heavy, sweet, warmth felt exactly the same way as the skirt material beneath his fingers. And beneath it, was Marnie. He squeezed and was rewarded with a "Mmmmmmm," which vibrated against his tongue.

It was beyond his capability to absorb the sensations all at once, so Zach concentrated on one thing at a time—the feel of Marnie beneath his hands, the taste of her mouth, the familiar smell of her shampoo and the sound of her breathing as she kissed him.

It was a great plan which would have set him up for a lengthy session of enjoying being with her, of sensual kissing and staying in the moment, but as usual Marnie had something to say.

"I think we've covered this territory pretty thoroughly, don't you?" She gently released his face to smooth her hands down his neck and shoulders.

"What do you mean?"

"I mean I've been thinking about you nonstop since last night."

"Glad to hear I'm not the only one."

She smiled. "You've been thinking about yourself?"

"Yes." Zach cradled her between his thighs. "Thinking that I didn't want to stop. Didn't want to leave."

"Hmm." She trailed one finger across his collarbone and down the center of his chest.

He was sure he hadn't taught her that move, either.

"Now where did we leave off? Oh, I remember." Holding his eyes with hers, she unbuttoned his top shirt button, then the next one down.

And Zach took a step back. That was as much as he could stand and not make love to her.

And it would be making love, he at last admitted to himself. She'd come into his life all at once, so it didn't surprise him that love had come quickly, too. He knew it was too soon for her to hear it and believe it, though.

"You pulled away last night, too." She dropped her hands. "Am I doing something wrong?"

He shook his head.

"What, then?"

"Don't you remember what I said?" His voice sounded as raw as he felt.

"That I shouldn't unbutton your shirt—"

"Unbutton, unbuckle, unhook or unsnap—"

"Unless I planned to get naked."

"Yeah." He could barely speak. "So what are we doing here, Marnie?"

She gave him a look that he'd remember for the rest of his life. "I guess I'm getting naked." She tugged at the hem of her top and before Zach could react, she'd whipped it over her head and tossed it in the air where it landed on a small antique lamp table.

The lamp may have wobbled and it could have crashed to the ground for all Zach cared. Marnie stood in front of him naked except for a black skirt and red toenails.

He couldn't breathe. He couldn't think. He couldn't move. "That's a good look for you," he said roughly, trying not to leap at her.

"Then why are you over there, when I'm over here?"

Zach didn't know, and he couldn't figure it out since his brain had ceased to function. All the blood had pooled into the part of his anatomy that needed it the most.

Telling himself—ordering himself—to go slow, he took a step toward her.

"Oh, don't bother," she said.

She'd changed her mind. He nearly walked over to the fireplace to get one of the tools and cause serious damage to Franco's lovely, antique-filled Victorian apartment.

"The bedroom is this way." Marnie, her back to him, walked away.

Franco's apartment was saved.

Zach almost didn't follow because the picture Marnie made, wearing nothing but the skirt was also something he'd remember, or hoped he'd remember, since his brain had shut down. That skirt was something else. It molded itself to her legs and caught the light in a way that made him start to shake.

Marnie stopped in the doorway, propped an arm on the doorjamb and turned so he could see the profile of one breast. "Coming?"

"Not if I stay out here." But he didn't move. Couldn't move. Probably because there was no air getting into his lungs. Because he wasn't breathing. Because he couldn't.

"Maybe this will give you some incentive." Marnie reached under her skirt and shimmied out of a pair of lacy barely-there hot-pink panties. Then she shot them across the room.

The unexpectedness of it made Zach inhale sharply, which solved the lack-of-oxygen problem. Ripping his shirt off as he strode toward her, Zach had unbuckled his belt by the time he reached the door. Marnie, laughing, ran inside the bedroom.

It seemed like forever since he'd given her the foot rub in here. She was standing so still now, staring at the bed. Maybe she was having second thoughts. Zach didn't want her having second thoughts while he wasn't capable of having first thoughts.

He stepped up behind her, trying to marshal a coherent sentence that would be appropriate. Placing his hands on her arms—certainly they wanted to be elsewhere, but he restrained himself—he said, "Marnie..."

She started laughing. Then she was pointing and laughing. "Zach, look! The bed's turned down."

"What's funny about that?"

"Look at the pillow."

Zach stepped closer and saw two square chocolate mints on either side of a rose. Nestled in the petals was a condom.

"That explains that," Zach said.

"How about explaining it to me?"

"When I passed Franco downstairs, the only thing he said was, 'Did you plan for this?' and I said, 'No,' and he said, 'Fortunately, I have.'"

"Wow. It's a good thing I didn't bring Barry in here."

From behind, Zach wrapped his arms around her waist and pulled her back against his chest. "Yeah, 'cause I would have broken down the door if you hadn't answered it."

"Good." She picked up a tent of paper from the nightstand, opened it and made an exclamation of delight. "Wednesday-Thursday is out of town."

"What does that mean?"

He nuzzled her neck and Marnie turned in his arms until she faced him. "It means late checkout for us. Let's see...I've unbuttoned, you've unbuckled—" She pulled at the waistband of his jeans until it popped open. "Now I've unsnapped and unhooking tonight was irrelevant. I think you forgot unzip."

Zach took her hands and looped them around his neck before kissing her. "It's too early to unzip."

He moved his hands to her breasts and was tracing

the outer edge of her lips with his tongue when she spoke, causing interesting sensations.

"Wha—what happens if I unzip now?" She was breathing quickly. He liked that.

"We have hot sweaty sex instead of long," he kissed her mouth, then her chin, "slow," he kissed her throat and the hollow below it, "sensuous," he kissed her chest and the top of her left breast, "sex," and he took the tip into his mouth.

Marnie gasped and clutched at his hair writhing quite gratifyingly.

And then he felt his zipper give way.

"Ma—" Not only had she unzipped his jeans, she was completely and totally naked, the skirt in a pool at her feet. "Marnie," he tried again. "You're—"

"Naked. Yes, I know. Try to keep up, okay?" She climbed onto the bed. Zach's jeans were off before she made it to the center.

Then he was on top of her, holding her hands above her head as he laced his fingers through them a second after that. He looked into her eyes, whispered, "You're beautiful," made sure she knew he meant it, then kissed her.

The passion simmering between them became a rolling boil. They couldn't get enough of each other, feverishly placing heated kisses wherever they could. Someday, Zach wanted to leisurely explore every part of Marnie's body, learning what made her moan and sigh and move her hips. Now, everything made her moan and sigh and move her hips and he felt the same way. All she had to do was touch him—anywhere. An elbow. A knee. His calf. And after a while, she didn't even have to touch him.

Her skin, her hair, her expression, the little gasps, her scent—Zach absorbed all of it. He wanted to absorb her and discover her essence, the part that made her Marnie, the part that was irresistible to him.

He watched her and all the expressions of passion that crossed her face. But it was the tiny little smile of feminine satisfaction that curved her lips when she explored him with her hands that sent him to the edge.

Zach knew he was on the brink, knew he wasn't going to be able to hold back any longer. "Marnie..."

Panting, she opened her eyes, saw his expression, then reached above her head and handed him the rose.

He inhaled, knowing that he would never again smell roses without thinking of her, and pulled a few petals out sprinkling them over her breasts and stomach.

"You're beautiful," he said, covering himself, then thrusting inside her.

He waited, allowing her body to get used to him, watching her eyes widen, then crease at the corners as she smiled. Taking one of the petals, she crushed it between her fingers and held it to his nose. It was a stronger scent, now. Earthier.

"This is beautiful," she whispered.

He smiled and she pulled him to her, wrapping her legs around his waist. "*You're* beautiful," he said again, and he kept saying it until she cried his name and he couldn't speak because he was shuddering his own release.

They lay in sweaty aftermath with the scent of crushed rose petals mingling with the scent of their bodies.

Marnie heaved a great sigh. "There wasn't an earthquake was there?"

Zach raised himself on an elbow. "Just ours. You're beautiful," he added.

"You keep saying that." Marnie lazily traced her fingers over his ear.

"I want you to believe it."

"I'm getting there." She grinned. "But I need more convincing."

"Oh, you do, do you?" He leaned in and kissed her.

"Definitely more convincing."

"We've got all night."

Marnie fumbled with something above her head and showed him a battered silver square. "Better than that, we've got chocolate."

Zach took the square and grinned. "That's not chocolate. It's a chocolate-flavored condom."

10

THERE ARE TIMES when it is best to forego a strict chronicling and indulge in reality fiction. Having set the stage, I have no compunction in doing just that for M. and Mr. R.'s night together.

MARNIE NEEDED lots of convincing so consequently, she didn't get much sleep. She woke up later than usual, but still with plenty of time to creep from the bed, tug her arms through Zach's shirt and call into work. She could have called in sick, but she'd never felt better—how could she lie about being sick? She took a personal business day, since she had a jillion of those to her credit. Then for good measure, she took Thursday off as well.

And now to get back to her very own personal business. She wondered whether or not to put the coffee on or even if they'd be drinking it before it got cold again.

She did check the fridge, wondering if Wednesday-Thursday had anything she could borrow. Not much. She'd have to run to the store while Zach checked on things at the site.

When she passed through the parlor, Marnie looked out the bay window to the house across the street.

Talk about a short commute. She grinned. Looked like she was about to have her first nooner.

Marnie's bare feet were getting cold on the floor. Good incentive to get back to bed. She already knew Zach was an excellent foot warmer.

When she got back to the bedroom, Zach was awake, already in his jeans, sitting on the edge of the bed and checking his pager. "Hey, I missed you." His voice was warm and sexy morning-rough. But Marnie noticed that he didn't look up from the little black pager.

Stop it, Marnie. "I'm cold!" she squealed and launched herself onto the bed, her momentum knocking Zach backward. Laughing she climbed on top and started kissing anything she could reach—and she could reach a lot.

She felt the rumble of Zach's laugh as she kissed his chest and reveled in the way he one-handedly hauled her up his body until he could kiss her mouth. Marnie was profoundly happy. She'd craved a relationship like this, sharing emotional and physical intensity with a man. During the night they'd talked and dreamed and made love, and she let herself fall *in* love, believing that their feelings were strong enough to handle the inevitable bumps in the road.

In Zach terms, they'd built a solid foundation. In Marnie terms, she'd found a man who'd put her first in his life. Hadn't he abandoned the house and followed her to the restaurant because he'd been worried about her with Barry? Here he was, devastated by the cancellation of the renovations, but he'd still thought of her.

Marnie sighed into the kiss and unsnapped the waistband of his jeans. He wouldn't be needing these—

A shrieking sounded in her ear. "Do you have an alarm on your pants or something?"

"My pager." He still held it. "Hang on."

Marnie felt him struggle to sit up and slid off him, her ear still ringing.

Zach studied the message, then stood. "I've got to get across the street."

Marnie felt cold. "It's...it's not even seven yet."

"It's that late?" He blinked and ran his hands through his hair. "Hey, you're wearing my shirt."

Marnie climbed beneath the covers before taking it off. Zach had gone looking for his socks and work boots. He came back into the bedroom, leaned down and gave her a quick kiss before shrugging into the shirt.

"I...I took the day off." Her lips were cold, too.

"Oh." He looked distractedly around the room. "I'll, uh, I'll try to get back over here."

Marnie gave him a suggestive smile. "Shall I wait for you here?"

The bed tilted with his weight as he sat on it to put on his socks and boots. "It might be a while. I need to keep an eye on things over there."

"All they're doing is putting plywood over windows."

Zach reached over and gave her a quick kiss. "It's a little more complicated than that."

Marnie smiled with determined brightness. "Lunch?"

Zach hesitated. "Lunch sounds good." He kissed her again and managed to convey regret as he broke it. "Don't get up. I want to think of you this way."

And he was gone. Just like that. Marnie tried to chalk it up to morning efficiency instead of morning-after abruptness, but couldn't quite succeed.

Okay, she was *not* staying in the bed because that would make her think and she would think the worst and she wasn't going to do that.

What she was going to do was get dressed, check her e-mail and walk to the grocery store to buy something terribly romantic for lunch.

Maybe she'd do a Google search for "romantic lunch recipes." Breakfasts were romantic. Dinners were romantic. Lunches were...lunches could be sexy nooners. Yeah. Zach would be desperate for her by noon. And naturally, he'd want to shower, so she'd better get some fresh towels from Franco.

And she'd better hurry because maybe Zach couldn't wait until noon....

In the end, Marnie raced around, shopped, managed to get towels from Franco without telling him anything—a massive accomplishment—but then again, he probably knew what she had to tell. He was quite pleased with himself, too, and she left him happily transcribing his notebook into the reconditioned laptop she'd given him. He was probably making everything up, but Marnie didn't care.

She bought enough food for dinner as well as breakfast. It was difficult, since she didn't cook much. She'd decided on pasta and salad for dinner complete with wine and candles, but lunch was tricky. It couldn't be heavy, but had to sustain a construction worker. She didn't want sandwiches because he probably ate them every day. Quiche had bad connotations. In the end, she went with a frozen chicken and rice casserole that could be microwaved since lunch's timing was up in the air.

So by ten-thirty, Marnie was ready and took her laptop to the desk next to the bay window to finally check her e-mail. While it downloaded, she could watch across the street and look for Zach.

He drove off and came back once and she saw that he'd changed clothes—and the khaki pants and shirt weren't work clothes, either. She smiled in anticipation and logged on to his Web site, played with the colors and tweaked things here and there. There had been a gratifying number of page hits and she studied the data to see which pages were viewed longest and how long the average surfer stayed at the site.

Her stomach rumbled and she looked at the computer clock, surprised to see that it was well past noon.

Zach's Bronco was still parked across the street and another car was there, too.

She sighed. He was meeting with someone. She checked her e-mail again, then on a whim, checked for e-mail sent to the Web master of Zach's site and was surprised to find a half dozen messages. She should have checked more often, but she wasn't used to getting e-mail from her sites since there was rarely anything wrong.

Is the e-mail for Renfro Restoration valid? I have sent three messages without reply.

The other messages were similar. Marnie knew

Zach wasn't on the computer much, but she was going to have to remind him to check his e-mail. He'd probably forgotten about this new account she'd set up for him. She logged on and was stunned at the number of inquiries and messages. She was going to have to tell him about this when he got here.

It was nearly one-thirty when Marnie decided that she could make a container of food and bring it across the street to him and after two before she got up enough nerve to carry it across the street.

Except the Bronco wasn't there.

Marnie stared out the window. She would *not* call him. She would *not* page him. He knew she was over here waiting.

The Bronco was back the next time Marnie looked. Still she waited, the hole in her heart growing larger with each passing minute.

By four o'clock, Marnie knew she'd made a mistake about Zach and was furious with herself. Hadn't she spent hours of her girlhood staring out the window as she waited for her dad? She'd recognized Zach as the same type and yet she'd let herself be sucked into the same cycle of anticipation, disappointment and broken promises.

Forget it. She was going to make a clean break. She logged back on to Zach's Web site to forward all Web master mail to his other e-mail address because she wasn't about to go back to that site ever again.

She was caught looking at it for a moment as the pictures she'd taken flashed by. Her eyes blurred when she saw the one of Zach in front of the "trompe l'oeil" house, his face radiating joy. Zach.

Marnie bit her lip. Hard. Time enough for crying later. Resolutely wiping her eyes, she scanned the e-mails before forwarding them.

The word *bed-and-breakfast* caught her eye and her mouth opened as she read more carefully. This was from the owners of that house Zach wanted to redo. The big one. His dream project.

He was going to be thrilled. She shook her head. At least one of them would be happy. Marnie printed out the e-mail before forwarding it and turned off the computer.

The weather was finally warmer so she put on one of her new sweaters, shoved the printout into her pants pocket and went downstairs to confront Zach. She looked good. She knew she looked good.

But the workers didn't whistle at her. She shouldn't have noticed and it shouldn't have mattered, but it did.

There was a different car parked out front, which meant Zach probably had visitors, but Marnie wasn't in a mood to put this off. Oh, she'd be discreet—no public scenes—but she wasn't leaving until she'd said what she had to say. Then she could go home and shatter into tiny little abandoned pieces.

She heard voices coming from the parlor where she found Zach talking to a couple. He was still wearing the khaki pants and he'd rolled up his shirtsleeves. Their backs were to her.

"If we can't hire you, would you consider evaluating the property to see if it's worth renovating?" the man asked as Zach shuffled through photographs.

"We do like the location and because of the historical significance we'd prefer to restore," said the woman, "but if you won't be available, then we'll have to go with making it livable."

Zach rubbed the back of his head. "It would be a huge job." He handed the pictures back. "And you know I've wanted to do this forever. It will make a fabulous bed-and-breakfast. But I can't right now."

"At least come look at the property," the woman said. "Maybe you'll fall in love with it, too."

"I'm already in love," he said.

Marnie must have made a sound because he turned around, his face lighting up when he saw her. It would have to be the exact same expression of joy she'd just seen in his picture.

"Speaking of..." He gestured for her to join them.

Feeling awkward, but knowing she was going to have to fake it, Marnie walked forward. Zach draped his arm around her. "This is Marnie LaTour, my Web mistress." He managed to make "Web mistress" sound sexy. "Bill and Charlene Nichol are buying the big house on the hill I showed you."

"Your dream-project house?"

"Yeah, I always thought I wanted a crack at it."

"Oh!" Marnie dug out the e-mail. "I've got your e-mail right here. I just found it," she said to the couple. "I apologize. I hadn't checked that account."

"Zach explained when we finally talked to him on the phone," Charlene said.

He smiled down at Marnie. "I forgot that you'd set up that other account."

"That's what I thought. Sorry. I should have kept up with it."

He dropped a light kiss on her temple. "You had other things to think about."

And still did. Except... "Did I hear you turning down the project?"

"Yes, he did." Bill looked unhappy. "If you have any influence, I'd be grateful if you'd use it to change his mind since I'm not sure we'll go through with the purchase if Zach's not on board."

"Zach!" Marnie looked up at him in astonishment.

"Yeah, I know." But he didn't look too unhappy. "It's timing and finances. I already accepted another job with an upfront bonus. I needed the cash because...this wasn't how I planned to tell you, but I bought this house today." He smiled crookedly at her. "For us."

So that's what he'd been doing. The hole in Marnie's heart filled with love again.

"Zach!" Marnie flung herself against his chest and burst into tears. She was as surprised as when she'd cried in front of Franco.

"She really likes Victorian houses," Zach said to the Nichols.

"Come on, Bill. We should leave them."

"If you change your mind..." Bill said.

Marnie swiped at her eyes. "Yes. He's going to change his mind."

"Marnie." Zach tilted her chin. "It's okay. Restoring this house for us to live in is my dream job now. And with the other project, there just isn't time for a massive job like the B and B."

"We'll work something out." She turned to the Nichols. "He will be in touch. This is going to work."

Zach waited until they were gone before saying, "Marnie, you shouldn't have told them that. There's no way."

She pushed herself off his chest and dug in her pocket for a tissue. "If you had talked to me about it instead of letting me sit there and wait on you all—day—long—"

"It took longer than I thought. I wanted to surprise you."

Marnie wiped her eyes and nose. "I used to wait on my dad. He'd always tell me it would be just a few minutes and I'd always believe him and then wait by the window for hours and then he'd promise to make it up to me and never would... Today was just like that."

"Aw, Marnie." He gathered her to him. "I didn't know. I should have called you."

"Yeah. I came here to break it off with you. I can't live with someone who's always putting other things first."

"I can't do that to you. I love you. I'm besotted with you. Frankly, it's been bordering on obsession—thinking about you with Barry made me crazy."

"Barry's a jerk. He was never anything."

"I'm glad because you're the best thing that's ever happened to me, Marnie. After last night, all I could think about was building a place worthy of you." He looked suddenly stricken. "I should have asked you whether you liked this house."

"Yes, you should have."

"I just assumed...I've got to stop doing that. We can sell it."

And right then, Marnie felt the last of her doubts melt away. "We can keep it on one condition."

"Name it."

"The wallpaper in this room looks like something a dog threw up. How about you restore the house to just *before* they put the wallpaper up? Bare walls? Okay? Please?"

He grinned. "I found another wallpaper in the layers and it goes much better with the blue and white tiles in the fireplace. It's Chinese influence. If you like it, we can use that. If not, anything else you want."

"You might regret saying that."

He kissed her. "I regret nothing."

"Your dream job?"

"Doesn't matter. It's not as important to me as it once was. You once told me I hadn't met the right woman. Now, I have."

Marnie looped her arms around his neck and kissed him. "You hungry?"

"For you, definitely."

"I was thinking food. I haven't eaten all day."

"Neither have I." He laughed. "I remember being promised a special lunch."

"Yeah, well, now it's going to be a special dinner."

Arm in arm, they walked outside.

As they passed by the workmen, she asked, "Zach, why didn't your crew ever whistle at me?"

"You're beautiful." He kissed her temple.

"Answer the question."

"Because I ordered them not to whistle at my woman."

"Am I your woman?" Delighted, Marnie snuggled against him.

"Yeah. I want you in my life, Marnie. I can't imagine you not being in it. And I want to be in yours. I want our lives all tangled up together."

"Does that mean I get to give you business advice?"

"Sure. Do I have to listen?"

She swatted at him. "You'll want to listen to this. While you were busy planning our future and turning down dream jobs, you failed to consider that I might want to invest in our future, too."

"I didn't mean to cut you out." He laughed. "I wanted everything settled so I could spend more time with you. I *really* didn't like getting out of bed this morning."

"And I *really* didn't like you leaving."

"You know, you'll always come first, but I do have a lot of work ahead of me."

"Hire help. Take the B and B job. That's my advice."

He drew his knuckles along her cheek. "Can't afford it."

"*I* can."

"Renovation is *very* expensive." He smiled in a way that might have been a little patronizing. Just enough patronizing that Marnie enjoyed wiping the smile off his face.

"You know, Zach, I'm also very good at what I do. I'm very well paid." She told him what she made and watched his eyebrows go up. "And, I've been living with my mother and paying her a minuscule amount of rent and have virtually no living expenses—except for a recent addiction to pedicures—so I've been saving and investing. And in spite of the ups and downs of the stock market, I've managed to do okay." She told him just how okay.

His face went blank. She could see him mentally adjusting to the concept. "How much?"

She told him again. "It doesn't seem real to me either. Just a bunch of numbers."

"A big bunch."

They'd reached the bottom steps outside the Victorian apartment building. "You think big enough to hire you to finish our house and find a competent assistant for you?"

He looked down at her. "Marnie, I can't let you do that."

She nodded. "I know, male pride and all that. Got any more token protests?"

"That's the only one. You have any idea what that Chinesewall paper is going to cost?"

Marnie laughed and Zach swept her into a huge hug and a thorough kiss.

"You realize Franco is watching?" she murmured against his mouth.

"Probably videotaping."

"Are you thinking what I'm thinking?"

"Something like this?" Zach grinned and swept her back in an old-fashioned movie clinch.

"I love you, Zach. Make it look good," Marnie said.

And he did.

Epilogue

AND ONCE MORE, the skirt works its magic for another couple. I have seen it firsthand, and yet I do not know how the magic works. I have never told M. about its special properties, and I don't think I shall. It makes for a more dramatic script this way.

Mr. and Mrs. Renfro have rented my apartment until their house is livable. It shouldn't be too much longer. I can only assume that the skirt apparently influences the speed of construction as well.